I Close My Eyes

By

Regina Puckett

1

Chapter One

"You do know that even though your eyes are closed others can still see you."

Annoyed someone was interrupting her much needed moment away from the stifling crowd, The Lady Jane Blackmore closed her eyes tighter and pretended to be anywhere but in the Braxton's ballroom.

The whole point of hiding in a corner at the back was to regain her composure, so why didn't this stranger just go away like any true gentleman would?

Even as she wished this, a warm shiver ran down Jane's spine, tempting her to take a peek at who owned such a deep and passionate baritone voice.

The entire night had already been a complete disaster. The last thing she needed now was another difficulty, and being caught with this stranger would most definitely fall into that category.

When searching out a good place to which to sneak away, she hadn't seen anyone hiding in this quiet corner of the ballroom. Jane had really only had enough time to note that the column here was suitably broad enough and the potted ferns growing about it full enough to hide her yellow gown.

And why hadn't the highly polished floor already

opened up and swallowed her? Jane had certainly prayed hard enough for it to do so.

The stranger cleared his throat.

"Shush," she hissed, immediately horrified at being so rude, but then Jane's eyes flew open of their own accord. She pressed the tips of her fingers against her lips and finally dared meet the smiling brown eyes of the rich baritone voice's owner.

Oh my. For the first time in her life she understood the benefits of a good swoon. If only she could carry such a thing off without making an even bigger fool of herself.

"Did you just shush me?" The stranger bit at his bottom lip, as if to suppress a grin. But the man had such a kind face, she doubted he could have stopped his perfect mouth from doing so even if he had wanted to.

His only imperfection appeared to be a jagged scar that ran from the corner of his mouth to the bottom edge of his left ear. It was still angry and red, so how could Jane not notice and stare? She immediately regretted it, for it brought the man to draw his perfect lips to a thin line as he self-consciously fingered the scar. When she continued looking, he crossed his arms, as though to keep from touching it.

Jane squeezed her eyes tight shut again and once more silently pleaded that the floor just this once swallow her whole. In this year of eighteen-twenty-five, this was the first ball of her third social season, and it was going as she had expected—horribly. She blamed her father. After all, she had repeatedly begged him to let her join a convent.

"But I want babies," she thought she'd only said to herself.

"Shouldn't someone formally introduce us first?"

Mortified beyond belief, Jane opened her eyes, despite every instinct telling her not to. All those seemingly wasted years memorizing how to behave in public. Her stepmother was surely going to be disappointed in her conduct when she found out, and find out she would. She always did.

Careful not to lean out too far from the ferns, Jane angled towards the man. There was the ever present danger of her stepmother discovering her hiding place, and Jane wasn't certain she had what it took to face the harsh judgements of her or the other fashionable guests, not so soon after having so mortifyingly fallen into the punch bowl.

"Did I say that out loud?" she whispered, but not low enough to mask her embarrassment. She hung her head and stared at the toes of her white satin slippers. Their once pristine state was now marred by the black marks inflicted on them by the ever-so-sweet but rather clumsy Viscount Wellington.

Her toes still ached from her one and only dance of the evening. It was hard to hold it against the poor man that he danced like a blind ox. Viscount Wellington was all bones and loose limbs. Even though the man meant well, he would never be graceful, no matter how hard he tried. It had only been his kind-heartedness that had weakened her enough to accept his request for a dance. The marring of her slippers had therefore been a foregone conclusion once she had pencilled his name onto her dance card.

"You have the scent of lemons," he observed.

Jane lifted her sleeve and sniffed. "I'm afraid so. Countess Braxton is well known for her wonderful punch. She certainly doesn't skimp on the sugar. I was so looking forward to having a drink before..." She flipped her fan open and stared at the floor. "Well, you know."

"It's a shame, then, that you spilled most of it."

Jane let her gaze meet his smiling eyes. "But at least I caught the bowl before it hit the floor."

The stranger did a slow inventory of the front of

her ball gown, one that sent a flash of heat coursing from the top of her head to the tips of her toes. Her once beautiful pale yellow gown was now a disgrace, splattered with punch. If he had only seen her before her unfortunate accident at the refreshment table, but then, the way he stared at her now was almost as though he didn't care.

Jane fanned the harder, hoping her cheeks didn't appear quite as red as they felt hot.

When the handsome stranger finally met her eyes again, he grinned. Jane only fanned as hard as her tiny wrist would allow, although in no way did it alleviate the heat that still suffused her face. She lifted her long black curls away from her neck and stared longingly at the closed French windows.

It would be heavenly to step outside and walk through Lord Braxton's rose gardens. They were said to be among some of the finest blooms in England.

That thought was short-lived, though, for her new friend had moved towards her a couple of steps, thankfully still being careful they both remained hidden.

Jane knew why she was hiding here, but why was this attractive man here with her, away from the most elite people in all of England?

But of course, she reasoned, no doubt there were overbearing mothers amongst the assembly who were trying to press an ugly daughter on him. Jane could only imagine how annoying it would be, for there were so many hideously greedy women trying to ensnare the rich and titled for their daughters. Even if this man wasn't so rich, and perhaps not titled, he was certainly handsome enough to have to run such a gauntlet.

Once more, Jane closed her eyes, but this time pictured this handsome stranger leading her in a waltz. He didn't look the type who would step on her toes. She could just see them both twirling in circles—around and around—one of his hands resting on her waist, the fingers of his other entwined through hers.

She smiled at that thought.

"No matter that you've closed your eyes again, I can still see you." He cleared his throat. "You're extremely lovely when you smile."

A warmth pooled in the centre of Jane's stomach. It made it even harder to meet his eyes again but she finally did. After all, she didn't want him thinking she was a complete ninny. Just because accidents happened wherever she went, it didn't mean she was a girl just out of school who didn't know the simplest of things about the social graces.

"Please, do be a gentleman and go away." Janes tried her best to cover the punch stain on her bodice even though it ran down most of the front of her once lovely gown, not to mention its stickiness that had already plastered her corset to her breasts in a most uncomfortable manner. She hated appearing so dishevelled in front of someone so unnervingly handsome. Why couldn't fate be kind to her at least once in her lifetime?

Jane had always dreamed of a night such as this, only without the punch bowl having been tipped over her gown. She had been to many balls but had never been asked to dance by any of the most eligible bachelors. They always stared past her, as if she didn't exist. The only gentlemen who ever asked her to dance were those like Viscount Wellington, those just as studiously avoided as she was herself. Many of them, though, seemed to prefer being bachelors for the rest of their lives in preference to considering her as a prospective bride.

Jane fingered the soft yellow fabric of the skirt of her gown. It was ruined—just like her life. She would never marry nor have children. Jane closed her eyes even tighter to keep the pain from consuming her. She drew in a deep breath and let her thoughts drift to the quaint little cottage by the sea that her mother had left her in her will. Jane would find a way to be happy there. After all, she had her books, but even more importantly, she would finally be rid of her stepmother. That thought in itself was enough to bring a smile to her lips.

When Jane opened her eyes, she found the stranger had moved yet further out of hiding.

"Get back before someone sees you," she hissed.

He took a step back but then glanced out from behind the column, at the other guests and the dancers.

He hissed back, "Maybe you should re-join the ball before you're missed."

Jane shrunk even further into her hiding place. "It's really better that I stay here. Just a little while longer. You ought to return to the ball before someone sees you here with me. It wouldn't do to set tongues wagging."

She tucked a curl of her hair behind her ear and stared at the floor. "You really don't want your name linked with mine."

"Now, how could I possibly know that if I don't know your name?" He stepped even further from their hiding place, now almost certainly visible to anyone who might look their way. Someone was bound to come over and enquire why he had chosen to be so removed.

"But there's no one here to introduce us, so I think you should run along before we're the cause of an awful scandal. I do hate scandals, especially when they involve me. My father has already warned me that if I give him cause for concern tonight it will be the death of him. And," she now whispered loudly, "I just can't be the death of my father."

"But what's life without a good scandal, eh? It would be terribly dull and stuffy."

His charming smile was enough to draw her gaze from his scar. He must have been the most dashing man in society before his otherwise perfect face was so noticeably marred.

Jane sighed. "It seems, though, that for some reason men can simply walk away from a scandal, far more easily so than a lady."

She snapped her fan shut and stood straighter. "I'm afraid my father will completely disown me if I do one more thing to cause an uproar tonight, certainly at Earl and Countess Braxton's ball. You have no idea how long a season can be when one is cause for ridicule and chatter at each and every event."

She stared at her satin slippers again. "I can't face another embarrassing season."

He snapped his fingers. "I know just thing."

Before Jane could do a thing, the stranger walked over to a group of nearby gentlemen. After a minute or two of discourse, he drew one aside. They stood with their heads together before finally coming over to Jane's hiding place.

She pressed even closer to the column and once more closed her eyes. How was it that each and every time she went out in public something horrible happened? As huge as the Braxton's London house was, how was it that she had managed to pick the only corner that had hidden a mad man? She was doomed. There was no way the three of them were ever going to go unnoticed now.

Jane might have remained close up against the column all night had she not recognised the deep resonating throat now being cleared.

Why couldn't he just go away? "Shush."

"Stop shushing me and open your eyes."

He clearly wasn't going to take the hint, and he was certainly no gentleman. Jane only opened her eyes again because she despaired that it was time to give up at last. She only hoped the nuns would be kind to her.

Her determined new acquaintance grinned before turning to his friend. "Robert, we have a slight difficulty that only a man of your good standing can help us with." The handsome stranger dipped his head to the other man. "Would you be so kind as to introduce the two of us?"

Jane knew Robert, but seriously doubted the viscount would know her own name. After all, he was first rate marriage material, so Jane had hardly ever been near the handsome man. It hadn't, though, precluded her from admiring Viscount Worthington's guileless, even if a mite too beautiful face. Never having been this close before, she had never noticed how brilliant blue were his eyes, stunningly beautiful but ever so kind. The viscount clearly thought his friend had lost his mind, but his good manners and gentle nature kept him rooted before Jane.

Over the previous two seasons she had kept a conceit: that the viscount had been her brother. She had often thought that if she had had an older brother he would have put a stop to all the vicious attacks she had had to endure since her coming out.

And now that he was standing in front of her, Jane saw that he was every bit the man she had always dreamed him to be. There was no hiding the strength of character in his eyes and in his confident demeanour.

Jane's make-believe brother bowed and then smiled. Deep dimples in his cheeks came out of nowhere, and if she hadn't before understood why all the unmarried ladies chased after him, in that moment she did.

"But, my dear Phillip," he implored, "the lady is far too lovely to draw into what is certain to become a scandal. We must escort her back to the dance floor before such a thing can happen." The viscount smiled at Jane, as if to apologize, but she knew that scandal seemed drawn to her every appearance in polite society. But the man who seemed intent on engineering her next one now gave a polite bow.

"And one of the many reasons," he grinned, "why we should hurry the introductions along."

Jane had become distracted by the way her dashing stranger's unruly dark curls fell into his eyes every time he bowed, although she did note a certain reticence held the viscount back.

"My good lady," he finally said, a smile lifting a

corner of his mouth, "if you would permit me to introduce my best friend, The Duke of Greystone. And,
Phillip, this is the beautiful Lady Jane Blackmore."

Jane couldn't help but blink at hearing the
stranger's name, although she tried to remain calm. It
had only recently come up in conversation, that after-
noon as it happened, whilst enjoying high tea at Lady
Harper's home.

Jane's gaze wandered back to the man's scar, her
interest piqued as to whether or not the rumour was
indeed true. But then here he stood in front of her,
his face scarred just as Lily had said it would be.

If Phillip noticed her staring, he didn't show it but
took her hand.

His devilish grin returned. "My friends call me
Phillip, and I think by now you should consider us
good friends, since we've shared such a special moment here behind Lord Braxton's ferns."

Jane's mouth fell open.

He grinned again. "Why is it we've never met?"

Trying to recover from her shock, Jane curtsied.
The Duke of Greystone? Her father was simply going
to kill her when he discovered she had made a total
fool out of herself in front of a duke.

She hoped by the time she met his eyes again her

expression would once more be the fake smile her stepmother had drilled into her since the vile woman had married her father, what now felt far longer than ten years earlier.

Jane glanced at the wet stain running down her yellow ball gown and then back at the duke. "Unfortunately, I seldom make it past the first dance before disaster befalls me and I have to leave."

The two men looked at her punch-stained dress but Phillip recover his good manners first. He took Jane's hand and kissed it. "Then the fault lies with me, because I should have been by your side to stop such a cruel disaster from ruining your night. I'll certainly make a point of doing so in the future."

It was a kind gesture and it did what it was clearly meant to do—Jane blushed again. "Thank you, but we both know this will be my last time out in public if we don't soon go our separate ways. Someone is bound to notice us huddled here in this corner. Please excuse me and I'll go find my father. I may as well accept defeat before he comes looking for me."

Jane didn't immediately leave, though, but flipped her fan open and yet again furiously fanned her hot cheeks. There was something rather marvellous about being surrounded by two handsome men. Why not enjoy these last few moments of freedom before being locked away in a convent, where she would no doubt die of either boredom or a rash from her woollen habit?

But then she looked over Phillip's shoulder and her heart sank, the best night she had ever had about to come crashing down around her ears.

Before either man could notice her distracted look, she pointed her fan over their shoulders and told them: "Gentlemen, you are about to meet my father, His Grace Stratton Blackmore, The Duke of Rutherford."

Chapter Two

"Your grace." Phillip bowed to hide his grin. The last thing he needed was for Jane's father to believe he thought this situation anything other than serious, but how could he not be amused at his own thick-headiness? After all, Jane had warned him several times he should have left.

If he had been a gentleman, Phillip would have just slipped away the moment she'd arrived. He had seen her heading to his quiet hiding place and so had had plenty of time, but common-sense had deserted him from the moment he'd seen her arrive on the arm of her father earlier in the evening. One moment he'd been evading scheming mothers and the next a glimpse of a yellow dress had stopped him completely dead in his tracks.

That gown was the loveliest creation he had ever seen on any woman. It clung to each and every curve of Jane's shapely body. If that hadn't been enough in itself to increase any man's hunger, the way her black curls swung with every move, revealing such a mouth-watering nape, would have reduced the strongest man's resolve, kept him glued to her every movement. Since then he had done nothing but daydream about pressing his lips to that spot where those black curls ended and her creamy skin began.

Whenever she had sighed, he too had sighed. Whenever she had smiled, so did he. Even as Wellington stepped on her toes, Phillip had winced in sympathy.

And as for Jane's apparent accident with the punch bowl, well, that had been anything but. Phillip had seen the whole sordid affair from his hiding place behind the fern-swathed column. After narrowly missing succumbing to yet another determined debutante's desire to dance, he had retreated to this chosen hiding place for a short respite. It had given him a clear view of the refreshment table, so when Violet Collins had pushed the punch bowl across the table, all he could do was watch Jane try to save the beautiful crystal bowl from dropping to the floor and shattering.

Phillip's first instinct had been to rush over and call out every man who had done nothing to assist the poor lady. Their society's supposed elite had done little but stand idly by, like common riffraff, sniggering at Jane's distress. He'd been incensed on her behalf, but before he could move, her posture had changed to one of resigned humiliation, leaving him open-mouth at her resilience. Her chin held high and with a fixed expression on her face, she had somehow navigated her way through the press of gawkers with such dignity that none dared meet her eye, never mind comment on her now ruined gown.

As Jane had made her way to the column behind which he was hiding, he had slipped around to its other side so she wouldn't be embarrassed by his presence, although this had put him once more in plain sight. Only when he had sneaked a look and found she'd closed her eyes did he then draw nearer, and so secrete himself once more. If he had been truthful with himself, he would have had to admit that he no longer had the power to leave, even had he tried, and so could do no other than remain rooted a little off to her side.

At first he had only been fascinated by her beauty, but while watching her struggle with her tears, something deep within him had stirred. Something he had never before felt, made all the stronger when she lowered her lashes, dazzling him with her serene nature. A quiet calm settled over her, as though the noise around them had simply faded away and she had gone to a calmer, happier prospect. Her transformation had been so beautiful to witness it had left him envious of her mettle and fortitude. How then could he possibly leave her alone without at least learning her name?

Phillip could even find it within his heart to forgive Countess Collins's dogged determination to draw his interest to her daughter, Violet. For without it he might not have sought out this peaceful corner of the ballroom, and the chance it had now given him to meet this bewitching lady.

Against such a pleasant thought, the prospect of a union with Violet's family, the Collins, brought a shudder running through him. The earl was a drunkard, one who, according to the rumour mill, enjoyed beating his womenfolk, and who had lately been gambling away most of the family's fortune. Unfortunately, the pig of a man reminded Phillip a little too much for comfort of his own recently departed father.

Unconsciously, Phillip rubbed along the length of his scar, taking him back to the afternoon he had received the disfigurement. Yeah, but he had had enough of drunks to last him a lifetime.

But then Phillip vaguely heard the loud clearing of a throat, and realised how lost in his own thoughts he'd become. He once again met the duke's thunderous glare, but couldn't help wondering at how he'd managed to reach the ripe old age of thirty years without ever once coming close to getting entangled with a woman. Tonight, though, he had a terrible feeling he had already crossed too many lines, and that his forthcoming choices would be whether to look for a second to accompany him at dawn or to become embroiled in the intricacies of a marriage contract. Although both should have worried him, the latter brought only a warm feeling of contentment.

"I beg your pardon, Your Grace. What were you saying?" Phillip hated appearing so inattentive, but it wasn't as though he had ravished the man's daughter. That thought, though, was enough to drag his gaze from The Duke of Rutherford's red and sweating face to the simply exquisite one of his daughter, to the eyes he'd somehow not as yet noticed were such an enthralling grey.

"I asked what you thought you were thinking when you accosted my unwed daughter, here amongst these ferns? It is patently clear you have no regard for your own reputation, Sir, but did you not once have consideration for my daughter's own?"

Jane stepped forward, placing her hand on her father's arm. "Please, Papa. You mustn't blame this gentleman. It was I who came back here to get away from the crush of the crowd. I had no idea this corner was already taken, otherwise I would not have intruded."

"But surely you could have sought me out, or found your stepmother, if you were in such need to leave?" He glanced at Jane's ruined gown. "Oh dear. Yet again, I see you've found a way to end the evening before it has even begun. Why is it that, no matter how hard your stepmother tries to teach you how to behave in society, you still fail so miserably?"

The duke gestured at Phillip. "And now you have the gall to add indiscretion to your long list of misdemeanours. Have you not brought enough shame upon our family already?" Then the man closed his eyes and muttered, "Why on earth couldn't you have been the son I so dearly wanted? At least then I wouldn't be standing here amongst my peers, trying to decide whether I need to run my sword through Radcliff, here, or bind my only child to a man who has, in cold blood, killed his own damned father."

Even in the noisy ballroom, the Duke's last condemnation sounded rather raucous. But then, perhaps the words only rang so loudly in Phillip's head, making it clear that his peers genuinely thought him the killer of his own father. Good. It would be better that way.

Relinquishing any defence against such a wrongful accusation, Phillip merely crossed his arms and waited. Afeared of Jane's true feelings, he kept his attention fixed solely on her outraged father.

Surely this farce of an evening would come to an end soon enough and he could go home. He longed for the solitude of his library and a refreshingly strong cup of his finest tea. At one time he would have been tempted by the thought of a large bottle of the best brandy, but having seen what it had brought his father to, Phillip had long since foresworn any such alcohol be allowed onto his properties.

The two men continued to stare at one another, each seeming to hope the other would vanish in a puff of smoke, but then Phillip finally said, "Do we really need to decide this here. I have no wish to give the gossipmongers about us any more fuel for their tittle-tattle? Perhaps we ought to negotiate any settlement by marriage in private."

Jane's gasp of anguish would have gone unnoticed had Phillip not been paying such close attention.

She seemed to recover quickly, though, immediately stepping between the two men. "I can't let you do this," she said to Phillip. You know as well as I do that nothing improper happened between us."

Her lashes lowered, covering her seemingly forever-changing eye colour. What Phillip had at first thought to be grey had become a pale blue, getting paler still as she'd become more distressed. He hated not being able to see them now, for they seemed the easiest way to gauge her innermost thoughts. Did she object because she didn't want him forced into an unwanted marriage, or because she had no wish of her own to be tied to a man such as him?

Then she caught him off-guard by saying to her father: "Can't we just go home?" She glanced around. "So far, no one else has noticed. Besides, we were but merely talking. No man should have his life ruined because I was hastily foolish enough to hide out of the way instead of seeking you out."

The duke hissed, "Of course someone has: your stepmother. She saw you both kissing and so sent me straight here, to force you to go home before you ruined us all."

Jane stumbled back, as though her father had slapped her, her hand flying to her mouth. "But she must have misseen." When she glanced over her shoulder at Phillip, he noticed her eyes were now a dark grey.

Although he so dearly wanted to place a comforting hand on Jane's shoulder, this would have raised her father's ire beyond recounting. Clearly, her stepmother had seen an opportunity to secure her daughter-in-law a husband, something his own foolishness had then delivered straight into the woman's hands.

Jane's father abruptly stepped forward, as if he might strike her, and without thinking, Phillip pulled her sharply to his chest, her glance at him saying he must simply have lost his mind. Phillip dearly hoped his smile appeared more reassuring than it felt. "Never mind, my dear. We've clearly been rumbled."

As he gently ushered her to Robert's safekeeping, his eye contact with his friend pleaded that he back up Phillip's subterfuge, despite Jane's startled protests. Then he clearly heard her whisper, "Nincompoop."

Fighting back an urge to laugh, he said to the

Duke, "So, may I suggest I follow you to your town-house, where we can settle everything this very night? My mother will be so happy to hear that Jane has finally accepted my proposal of marriage."

The duke turned to his daughter. "Is this so, Jane?" but then directed his sudden rage at Phillip. "Why hide your affections for my daughter when you could have settled this like a gentleman?"

"But Father," Jane said from beside Robert.

"Shush," Phillip hissed, then grinned at her exasperated huff.

"Did you just shush me?" she tried to say out of her father's hearing, then to make certain, stepped nearer and clandestinely elbowed him.

"Turnabout is fair play," he whispered back.

When she jutted her chin out and crossed her arms, Phillip couldn't help but laugh. He liked her pluckiness. Even faced with certain downfall, she was still ready to take on the world, singlehandedly.

He bowed his head, as though ashamed, but really only to hide his grin. "I have been a complete cad, Sir. I admit it. I pulled Jane in here to try and convince her to run off with me tonight, to Gretna Green. But before I had the chance, my good friend Viscount Worthington intervened, insisting I do the honourable thing by her and ask for your permission to marry your daughter, Lady Jane. We were on our way to find you when you instead found us."

Jane's father appeared anything but convinced. However reluctantly, he finally offered Phillip his hand. "Well, in that case, let us retire to my home, where we can discuss the marriage contract before the night is out."

Chapter Three

"Stop pretending to be asleep. You'll not get out of this scrape as easily as that." The duchess gave one long sniff that bounced around the carriage as though it had a life of its own.

Jane could think of no more annoying sound than her stepmother's constant sniffing. It gave the impression of her forever smelling something offensive to her delicate sensibilities, but then maybe the horrible woman really did smell such things. The unpleasant vapours of London on a hot summer's day and her stepmother's obnoxious perfume no doubt presented many such reasons.

At one time, Jane had been able to shut out the woman's barrages by merely closing her eyes, but these last few months it had become even harder to do so. Either Jane was finding it more difficult to conjure up those happy places she retreated to during such occasions or her stepmother had grown more determined to be heard.

Jane opened her eyes only to find what she had expected—both her father and stepmother glaring at her from the other side of the carriage. Why couldn't they give her a moment alone in her own head, so she

29

could try and fathom how her life had got so turned upside down? One minute she had been hiding behind a column, the next betrothed to a complete stranger.

Her first mistake had been catching the punch bowl instead of letting it crash to the floor. Certainly a lesson hard learned. More importantly, was marriage not too high a price to pay for simply speaking to a stranger? And why didn't anyone take into account that she had told Phillip to leave, before they could become ensnared in any scandal? Well, it served the man right that he was now having to marry her. He should have listened.

Jane found it too hard to look at her stepmother and not scream that she was a conniving liar, and so Jane again closed her eyes.

"Look at your mother when she speaks to you," said her father.

That was more than Jane could handle. She had tried her entire life to be an obedient daughter, but surely enough was enough. Clearly trying to do the correct thing was never going to be good enough for her father, and she would continually be blamed for whatever went wrong.

Jane met her father's glare with one of her own.

"She. Is. Not. My. Mother."

The duke shifted forward in his seat. "Do you suppose you are too old to be beaten? Until you have exchanged vows with that...that murderer, you are still under my authority. You will respect my good wife the duchess as long as you're under my roof, do you hear? I simply will not put up with your endlessly discourteous cheek."

Jane waited for her father to strike her, even silently dared him to, and was strangely disappointed when he didn't. What was wrong with her? Maybe if this one time she struck him, instead, it would then give him the excuse he was looking for to beat her, until he felt better, or better still, killed her. What did it matter, anyway? Her life was, for all intents and purposes, over.

Jane bemoaned having been so close to slipping out from under anyone's control. In just a few months' time she would have inherited her mother's property, become her own person in her own right, not some man's possession. But now, because of her own carelessness, she would be forever chained to one.

It was simply not fair. None of it was fair. But would it be so terrible being married to a man with such gentle eyes? And Phillip *had* stood up to her father. It took a very brave man to do that. No one else had come to her defence since her mother's death. It was silly, but for a moment Jane had felt safe.

She lifted her chin and met her stepmother's triumphant stare. So the witch thought she had won? Somehow, Jane would turn this horrible situation into something good, if for no other reason than to show this ghastly woman that she couldn't win every battle.

"Why did you lie to Father?" Jane asked her. "You know full well I never kissed the Duke of Greystone, and seeing you saw me with him, why did you not come over to see if I needed you? You had to know that Violet would do something to ruin my night. She always does."

"Are you going to allow your daughter to call me a liar?" The duchess elbowed her husband, but before he could speak, she lashed out again at Jane. "You should be ashamed of yourself for blaming all your own clumsiness on such a lovely girl. All Lady Violet Collins has ever done to you is be more beautiful and display better manners. You're only envious. Instead of accepting responsibility for your own actions, you once again try to cast your failings onto an innocent bystander."

Before Jane could reply the carriage lurched to a stop and the head footmen opened the door.

Jane's father slid forward, but before stepping out, he hissed, "You will hold your tongue and go directly to your room until I call for you." He climbed down from the coach and waited to assist his wife.

Jane's evil stepmother leaned forward and whispered one last threat, out of the duke's hearing: "You will do well to remember your place, my dear. You aren't married yet, so I wouldn't get above yourself just yet, certainly not before that happens. I can and will make your final days with us a living hell, if need be."

Jane would have given anything to slap the smug smile from her stepmother's face, but such thoughts she knew were fruitless. To do so would only enrage her father even more. She would have to accept her fate, making the best she could out of whatever was in store for her.

She sat back in her seat, arms crossed, her heart racing. Jane might have stayed there all night had the footman not discreetly cleared his throat and offered his gloved hand, which she took and climbed down. Just as she was straightening her skirts, another carriage rolled to a halt behind theirs.

No doubt it was the Duke of Greystone, come to meet his doom. Her stomach became nervously unsettled all of a sudden and so she turned for the front door, but she had only taken a couple of steps before a hand took her arm.

"Could we talk before I sit down with your father to discuss our marriage contract?"

Jane turned to face her future husband. Even in the dark, she thought him far too handsome for someone such as her.

"We really mustn't get caught out here alone. My father will be most displeased."

Phillip's laughter floated upon the night air like a beautiful whisper. "I can't imagine him being more displeased than he is right now."

Jane wrapped her fingers around the sleeve of his black dress coat. "I'm so sorry. All of this is my doing. You should go while there's still time. It will all blow over in a few days' time. There's no point in ruining the rest of your life for something as silly as getting caught talking to me unchaperoned."

Phillip only pulled her up against his chest, his breath hotly fanning her cheeks before his lips

34

brushed against hers. Her every thought abandoned her at this, her first kiss—well, almost a kiss. Their lips had touched but for a mere fraction of a second, enough, though, to shatter Jane's nerve. All she could do was hold her breath and wait.

"I only wanted to ask what you would want above all else from your father. As our forthcoming marriage is a forgone outcome, it should at least gain you what you would most desire. Just tell me and I'll make certain your father includes it in our contract of marriage."

"But you don't have to."

Phillip placed a gloved finger over her lips. "I insist. So, what should I ask of your father?"

"Very well," and Jane stomped her foot when he again touched his finger to her lips. "My dearest wish is that you can never say I didn't give you an opportunity to walk away."

"Consider it so. But hurry now, before your father sends a servant out looking for us. What is your real wish?" He tucked a curl behind her ear.

"In my mother's will, she left me a cottage in Dorset, one I'm supposed to inherit on my twenty-first birthday, but my stepmother has been scheming to keep it from me. She's determined that I have nothing of my mother's." Saying it aloud like this gave Jane such a sense of release, that at least someone else now knew of her fears.

The cottage by the beach wasn't large, but the memories of those peaceful times she'd spent there with her mother were still so vivid. Every year, until her mother's death, it had been just the two of them enjoying their swims in the chilly sea, their quiet strolls on the beach and the lovely nights sitting in the parlour, its windows wide open and the salty air blowing in through the delicate lace curtains.

Jane had often fallen asleep there, sitting beside her mother in the evenings as they listened to the sea rolling in onto the rocky shore. They'd needed little during those yearly visits, and so had only employed a married couple from the village to tend to their needs. The woman, Helen, had cooked and cleaned whilst her husband, Joseph, had taken care of the cottage and its grounds.

Jane and her mother had both flourished there, once out from under the ever judgmental and watchful eye of her father. So how could Jane let her stepmother take the one thing she had left of her mother? That place belonged to Jane and her memories—no one else.

"Where do you go when you close your eyes?" and Phillip this time ran his gloved finger along the curve of her cheek.

It wasn't until he'd asked the question that she realised she'd once again drifted away.

She finally met his eyes. "All I ask is for my mother's property. I promise. I know you weren't looking for a wife, so I'll think no less of you if you turn around right now and leave."

He kissed the end of her nose. "I know you weren't looking for a husband, either, so maybe there's a way for us both to make the most out of a bad situation."

Chapter Four

"Stop acting like a harlot and come into the house this instant. Isn't it bad enough you've already embarrassed your father in front all his friends this evening? Must you also sully the Blackmore name with our neighbours, as well?" Jane's stepmother stood at the top of the townhouse steps, staring out into the darkness at Jane and Phillip.

Phillip would have laughed at the woman's unnecessary attempt at chastening Jane, if not for the way Jane stiffened at hearing it. He would soon put a stop to that vile woman having any power to hurt her. As the wife of a duke, Jane would be as powerful as her stepmother. Phillip had never wanted to inherit his father's title, but maybe it would be useful after all.

While it was true he hadn't been looking for a wife, had he been, then he couldn't have made a better choice than Jane. She was everything he had dreamed his future wife would be. That was of course before he had made the decision never to marry and have children.

After his father's death, Phillip had pledged not to carry on the Radcliff name, but how to tell Jane that they would be married in name only? Was it at all fair to do such a thing, but then what choice had Blackmore left him? A tiny voice in the back of his mind whispered that he could just walk away. So why didn't he? The same voice, though, then told him it was because the moment he had seen Jane standing there with her eyes closed, as if she had shut out the entire world, had been when he had wanted her to open them and see him, and see what no one in the world had seen before—his soul.

He offered Jane his arm and grinned, hoping it would be some small reassurance that they would get through the strain of this evening together.

Jane lifted her chin and drew in a deep breath before taking his arm. She didn't return his grin, though, but she did nod, as though she understood the support he was offering, and which she then graciously accepted.

Together they approached the duchess, as if they were simply returning from an evening's entertainment. Their bravado lasted only as far of the top of the steps, where they then stood before her.

Her stepmother grabbed Jane's arm. "Go upstairs this instant and change out of your soiled gown. I would not wish the duke get the wrong impression about my adeptness at being a mother, even though it's clearly too late to keep him from getting the wrong impression about your morals."

The woman sniffed. "Of course, that's really not my fault. I did try to raise you better."

While he would have liked nothing better than to snatch Jane out of this woman's grasp, Phillip instead bowed. "Pray, worry not, Duchess. I am sure I am already acquainted with your aptitude for motherhood."

The duchess sniffed again, this time even louder, her nose retaining its unattractive wrinkle.

Jane and he walked in together, but at the foot of a staircase, Phillip stood and waited until Jane had disappeared into one of the first floor rooms before allowing the waiting footman to escort him to a set of large closed doors. The footman respectfully knocked and waited, as footmen do, whilst Phillip harboured tired resignation as he too waited.

This was not how he had intended his night to end. He had planned on making a courtesy call at the Braxton's ball before travelling on to his club with Worthington, for a quiet evening of cards. Worthington was the only friend he had who understood his reasons for not drinking spirits, and hence made his the only company Phillip could tolerate for more than thirty minutes at a stretch. His other friends thought it their duty to badger him into drinking like a "Real man". He forgave them, of course, for after all they had not been raised by a monster of a sot.

"Come in," the Duke gruffly called from beyond the closed doors.

Those words sent Phillip's stomach plummeting. So here was his moment of truth. Could he really marry a woman he had only met but three hours earlier? What else could he do, though? He certainly wasn't the sort to let a woman become ostracised by society because of his own stupidity. He had known, the moment he'd stayed rooted there in that dark corner with Jane, that her reputation might be tarnished if they were seen. But there he had remained, as though his life had depended upon it, as it now so plainly did.

Chapter Five

As Jane sat down in one of the chairs in her father's study, she stared at the paperwork on his desk. The sight of the neatly stacked papers sent a wave of chills down her spine.

She was to be married. There was no way out of it now. The whole time her maid had been helping her change her clothes, Jane had hoped something would be said here to change the outcome of this evening's debacle. After all, surely two reasonable men should have been able to think of a better way to end this bizarre night than to sign her life away as if it didn't matter. It seemed as though she was no better than a piece of horseflesh, one to be bartered away by mere signatures on scraps of paper.

"So it's settled then?" Jane swallowed past the rising bile and met her father's gaze.

"It is," her father said abruptly from where he sat at his desk, clearly sensing her outrage, for he quickly looked away.

Jane glanced at Phillip, lounging in a wingback chair furthest from the fireplace as though he'd not a care in the world. She couldn't blame him for his choice of chair, for the room was stifling. Why had her father ordered the fire be lit? Maybe he thought it would speed up this unpalatable meeting and so get him to his bed before dawn broke.

Jane's father stood. "The duke has asked to speak with you privately, and since the marriage agreement has been signed, I see no harm in it."

He turned and bowed in Phillip's direction. "I bid you goodnight, Sir, but request you leave as soon as you've had your say with my daughter."

He stopped at the study door and added, "John, my butler, will show you out," but then he met Jane's eyes again. "And you will behave as a lady, do you hear? Just because I've given my permission for the two of you to speak in private does not give license for any inappropriate behaviour."

The duke addressed Phillip directly. "But soon enough she'll be your problem, Sir, not mine and her mother's."

"That woman is not my mother." Jane clasped her hands together before her, to keep from raising her fist in protest. But then, really, what was the use? No one ever listened to what she said.

"You will mind your manners and show proper respect for the duchess. She's done nothing but sacrifice her time and good offices to help raise you when

43

she had no compulsion to do so. Why, I have no idea, since you've shown time and time again just how little you value her endeavours to turn you into a respectable member of society." With that the Duke of Rutherford had clearly washed his hands of his daughter, emphasised by the resolute way in which he closed the door behind him.

For some reason her father's speech had the opposite effect on Jane than intended. The moment the door closed, she started giggling, and each time she tried to stop, she only giggled louder. She covered her mouth and drew in a deep breath.

"I'm so sorry. You must think you're betrothed deranged," but then another giggle slipped out.

Phillip stood and came over to her, where she still sat, but then, to her surprise, he knelt at her feet.

"I think you've been through a lot tonight and are simply exhausted." He took her hand in his and entwined his fingers through hers. It was such a lovely sensation that it dispelled her desire to giggle.

"I know your father has given us permission to speak alone, but I feel we shouldn't linger. I am certain poor John has been instructed to see me off the premises before too much time is out, so let me get straight to what I need to say."

Just as Jane was getting used to having a complete stranger hold her hand, Phillip released it and stood. She stayed silent and waited, well aware that her fate was already signed and sealed. What else was there to do but what all women have done down the centuries? She accepted her destiny with a grim and heavy heart.

"I have done as you requested and had your father include your mother's inheritance in our marriage contract. Although I don't think your stepmother could ever have legally taken it from you, you were probably wise to be concerned. From what I've seen of her I wouldn't trust her, either." Jane nodded and Phillip then began pacing in front of the fireplace.

She could feel his unease and it only added to her own.

"I instructed your father to put the remainder of your mother's money on your personal account. I must say, I was surprised to discover it was well over fifty-thousand pounds. You alone will have control of what your mother intended you. The house and surrounding land in Dorset will soon be titled in your name, so you will never have to worry about your stepmother again."

Jane cleared her throat. "That is very generous of

you."

Phillip stopped pacing and faced her. "Wait to hear everything before you heap unworthy praise upon me."

His intense expression made Jane's stomach knot, and she clenched her fingers together.

"I have my own reasons for wishing you to be settled." He looked away, taking a deep breath.

"You may have heard rumours that I killed my father." He briefly met her eyes before looking over at the closed study doors. "I won't go into what happened that day of my father's death, suffice it to say..." He looked at her again. "Suffice it to say that I made a promise over his body that I would never bring a child into this world. My father's tainted seed stops here, with me. I'll not bring more needless sorrow into this world."

This was all too much and too fast for Jane to take in. Of course she was thrilled to hear that her mother's property would soon be hers, as she had wished, but what was he saying? What did he mean that he wasn't going to bring children into the world?

She stood and approached him, aware that it was now time to face her future like an adult, not as some obedient child whose own thoughts on the matter were of no consequence.

"I'm to be your wife in name only?" Jane searched his face but he looked away, as though hiding his shame.

She whispered, "Is that really to be my fate?" and she too now paced before the fireplace, trying to sort out her tormented thoughts.

What new shame was this to be? Childishly, she had hoped that one day she would finally have someone who loved her, if not a husband then maybe children. After all, would they not have loved her quite naturally, even if no one else did? But to hear she was doomed to a lifetime without such hope was too much to bear. It was a heavy price to pay for seeking out a quiet corner at the Braxton's ball, to gather her thoughts.

Phillip finally found his words, although he did not move, nor did he look at her. "I'll request a special license in the morning, so we won't need reading of the banns. When that's been issued, I'll call with a minister, my friend Viscount Worthington and my mother, to arrange a quiet service at your family's church. If you then go ahead and pack your things, I can send someone over to collect them and have everything taken to your place in Dorset, in readiness for when we've been wed."

He drew in a long breath, and as she stopped by his side, he rushed on, "I'll send my land steward to check on your house there, to make sure it's in good repair and to arrange that help is taken on before you arrive."

At last, he met her eyes. "Is there anything I've forgotten?"

"So you're not worried that my father may contest our marriage contract if we live separately? He won't be happy to learn of that."

She looked away. "Not that he cares about my feelings, but he will detest the gossip our permanent separation is certain to stir up amongst his peers."

Phillip took her hand in his. "I'll go down with you to Dorset, and when I return home will say it is to attend to business. Every now and then I'll return to you, to make certain your needs are being met. That should settle any gossip for now, and soon enough no one will think anything about us living apart. Married couples do it all the time."

"I see you have it all sorted." She withdrew her hand and tucked both behind her back, so he couldn't take one again. It was too much to expect her to be indifferent to him whilst he held her hand, as if he cared about her feelings. Clearly he did not. His scheme was too cold and calculated for her to believe that he felt anything for her. Maybe he was the kind of man who lacked such ability, to feel for another. Not that she would ever know anything about what her future husband felt, given they were to remain strangers.

To keep from being wholly swallowed by sadness, Jane closed her eyes.

Except for the sounds of the fire crackling and Phillip's breathing, the room remained silent. But as hard as she tried, she couldn't find the happiness she usually did when she shut out the rest of the world.

Finally, she settled on the thought that she would be no worse off than she had been planning all along. Wasn't this the life she had already decided for her future? Of course, without a husband, but at least it meant she didn't have to wait for her birthday in December legally to claim her mother's inheritance. So why did she feel so sad at the thought of doing it now?

Jane hated to admit that sometime over the last few hours she had secretly begun to harbour thoughts of how wonderful it was going to be to be married. It wasn't how she had envisaged it, though, of her becoming engaged, nor was it how she'd imagined meeting who was to become her husband. But whenever Phillip was near, he made he want something she had never wanted before—a man who cherished her.

Phillip ran a finger down her cheek and whispered, "Where do you go to when you close your eyes?"

Jane opened them and stepped away. "Sometimes I just have to run away, but then I open my eyes again and here I still am."

Chapter Six

Phillip was grateful that the days before the wedding had been filled with hurried preparations, all of which had helped his days pass in a blur. Making certain everything was taken care of for Jane's arrival at her cottage, seeing that her mother's money had been transferred to her account and transferring more from his own to ensure she wanted for nothing had taken most of Phillip's time. As his wife, she deserved whatever her heart desired, provided it never desired him.

It had all kept him from dwelling on the look on Jane's face when they'd parted company at the end of his, Robert's and the minister's visit to make arrangements for the service. He was a complete coward for having stayed away since, but he'd been unable to face her again, not until he would have to on the day of their marriage.

But when that day came, instead of a long-faced bride, as he'd feared, coming to stand in the church beside him, Jane surprised him by presenting a look of resolve. Phillip could hear the minister speaking but the man's words seemed to him but mere gibberish, so distracted was he. His mother was in the small congregation, but he avoided turning to see her look of displeasure, wishing for the hundredth time he hadn't told her of his plans to send Jane away to her cottage afterwards.

Phillip hoped Jane didn't think she could change his mind after their vows were exchanged. The truth was: Phillip didn't know what bothered him more, the thought that Jane was plotting to make him somehow fall in love her or that she was looking forward to a life without him.

A pain had grown in his chest since their last parting, one that now, standing here before the minister and both their families, only grew stronger and stronger. He almost felt bent from the burden of carrying it.

But just when Phillip thought his knees might give way, Jane reached over and took his hand. She squeezed his fingers and smiled. If truth be told, it wasn't much of a smile, but he saw it for what it was—a peace offering. So when it came time for him to say his vows, the words slipped out with ease, Jane's own soft promise to be his wife bringing him a relief he hadn't expected.

At the end of the short ceremony, when Jane closed her eyes and lifted her face for his kiss, Phillip hesitated for only a second, but long enough for her to open them again. Her beautiful grey eyes clearly pleaded that he not embarrass her in front of everyone, so he touched her cheek with his finger and smiled.

How could he not kiss her? She was his wife. Whatever that may eventually mean, for now he would truly be her husband. He had promised before God and those gathered to witness it that he would honour her before all others, and so he would. He would be hers, and hers alone, faithfully until the end of time. So he touched his lips to hers, to seal his silent vow as he prayed that this sweet woman wouldn't grow to hate him for what he was asking of her.

"You can let her come up for air now, my friend," and Robert's voice reminded Phillip they had an audience, so he reluctantly parted their lips and stepped back from Jane.

Robert clapped a hand on his shoulder. "So, how does it feel to be a married man?"

Phillip slipped his arm around Jane's waist, partly to steady himself, and took Robert's offered hand and shook it. He then drew in a deep breath as he looked at Jane, and before motioning for his mother to join them. "Mother, this is Jane," he said when she came beside them. "I told you she's lovely, didn't I?"

Phillip was unsure whether his mother would approve of Jane but was pleased when she pulled her into a motherly embrace.

The Dowager Duchess of Radcliff then stepped back, a hint of tears in her eyes. "Phillip has told me so much about you. You're just as lovely as he described. You have to know that I wish you both such happiness together."

Phillip tried to keep his tone light but a quiver revealed his sudden apprehension. "Mother, Robert was asking if I felt any different now I'm a married man. What do you think? Do I look any different?"

His mother patted the jacket sleeve of his fine wedding suit. "You've never looked more splendid. I think marriage suits you."

Even though his mother's words were meant only in kindness, they cut Phillip to the quick, knowing his marriage was secretly a sham. Somehow, it didn't feel right for her to heap praise on him when what they were doing surely went against what God had meant marriage to be.

To hide his misgivings, he smiled and turned to Jane. "So what do you think? Do you feel any different?"

Her face flushed prettily but she was clearly only putting on a brave face. "I don't know how married is supposed to feel, but I know I feel queasy."

Robert drew her away from Phillip and raised her hand to his kiss. "I think," he then said, "that pretty much explains how all couples feel about the state of matrimony—queasy."

The small group laughed but their merriment was cut short by Jane's father's rather censorious voice. "The servants will have the wedding breakfast laid out for our return. I hope you don't mind but we invited a few close friends who are in town and had no prior engagements to join us."

He cleared his throat before adding, "It's not the way the duchess and I would have wanted our daughter's wedding day to have been celebrated, but at such short notice it's the best we can do."

The duke turned to Phillip's mother, a gracious expression now fixed to his face. "It will be an honour to have you as a guest at my house."

He bowed, then offered his arm. "If you're ready, Lady Radcliff, I'll escort you to your carriage."

The dowager smiled at Phillip and Jane before accepting the Duke of Rutherford's arm and letting him lead her away.

Phillip glanced at Jane, to judge her reaction to her father's blunt rudeness, and was surprised to find her calm and composed. The years of living under Blackmore's censorious glare must have hardened her, but Phillip was outraged on her behalf. A daughter deserved a little sentimentality from her only parent on her wedding day. From what he had seen of her stepmother, he expected no well wishes from the selfish woman, but Jane should have been able to expect better from her father.

Phillip took Jane's hand in his and kissed her temple. "Are you ready to eat our first meal together as husband and wife?"

Now her father was out of earshot, she told him, "Truthfully, I'm not certain I can keep anything down. I wasn't joking when I said I felt queasy."

Robert leaned in and whispered, "Duchess, maybe you should try to eat a little something. The last thing you want is for our wedding guests to think your loss of appetite is because you're quickening."

Robert touched Jane's arm. "You know how rumours spread through society. With the two of you marrying so hurriedly there's bound to be talk that it's because you're with child."

Jane leaned her forehead against Phillip's shoulder and whispered, "Will there be no end to society deciding how I am to behave? Even at my own wedding breakfast, what I eat or don't eat seems determined by the tittle-tattle of its gossipmongers."

She looked into his eyes. "Please say we are leaving soon for Dorset. I have no desire to linger at my father's house one second longer than necessary."

She reached up and straightened his stock. "I can tell from your worried look that you believe you're doing me a disservice by taking me to mother's cottage and leaving me there."

She regarded her father's retreating back. "Truthfully, I'll be happier there than I could ever be here with people who despise my every action."

Jane took his hand in hers. "I'll never be sorry I married you, and I promise I'll try do nothing that would make you wish you hadn't married me. If everything we said here today, during our wedding service, were to mean nothing, let's promise each other that we'll find a way to be truly happy."

Chapter Seven

Jane rested her head against the side of the carriage and let its rocking motion settle her stomach. Strangely, it did seem to relieve some of her queasiness, but it hadn't done anything to help her pounding headache. It didn't really help that she could feel Phillip's stare. Now they were alone, they'd exchanged hardly more than a few pleasantries.

She feared her heartfelt speech before they had returned to her father's house for breakfast had unsettled him, instead of easing his mind as she'd intended. But what else could she do? She had tried her best to let him know she accepted their form of marriage. Was it how she had dreamed her life would be? No, but anything was better than the hate-filled atmosphere her stepmother maintained within her father's London house.

"Are you going to stare at me throughout the two days of our journey to Weymouth?" Jane said, opening her eyes and smiling, in the hope it would soften her question.

Phillip smiled in return. "But you're really very beautiful. I don't think I've taken the time properly to appreciate just how lovely you are."

He leaned forward. "So how is it you've made it to twenty years of age and never married? Has no one else looked at you as I have?"

His scrutiny made Jane feel uncomfortable, so she turned her gaze to the passing scenery. "I don't think anyone has ever seen me wear anything but a gown drenched in punch."

She looked at him, long enough to smile, before turning her gaze back to the view. "People see what they wish to see. Violet Collins has made it her sole duty to harass me at each and every ball I've attended since my first season."

"Why does she hate you so?" His voice held so much interest that Jane couldn't help but meet his gaze again, but she shrugged.

"A question for Violet Collins, not for me. I've barely spoken more than a couple of words to her, but the night of my coming out ball she tripped me before I could descend the staircase into the ballroom. And when that didn't stop me from attending, she upset her first bowl of punch over me. I think it amused the other guests so much she's continued gaining her fun at my expense."

Phillip shook his head. "Her mother has tried her best over the last few years to marry the two of us.

Their property adjoins my estate, so my father and Lord Collin discussed the two of us marrying whilst I was still a youngster, but fortunately nothing was ever drawn up."

He shuddered in spite of the heat. "I can't imagine what a marriage to such a mean-spirited woman would be like."

From what little Jane knew of Violet, she was sure she would never have settled for a marriage in name only, and she would certainly not have packed up all her earthly possessions and gone off to live alone in a small coastal village.

She kept this to herself, though, merely saying: "I suppose it's a good thing I picked your quiet corner to sneak off to, then. Violet can be very enterprising when she puts her mind to it, so I'm amazed she hasn't found a way to have you *accidentally* compromise her."

Of course, after saying that, Jane blushed, for if truth be told, hadn't that been exactly what she had done herself.

As if reading her thoughts, Phillip quickly changed the subject: "So what's your mother's cottage like?"

Jane closed her eyes and let her mind drift off to

the dunes and the dark blue waters that rolled onto its quiet beaches. If she tried hard enough, she could almost hear the wind blowing across the water as the surf rolled in.

A smile tugged at her lips as she tried to explain what the cottage meant to her. "It's like nothing you've ever seen before. There's happiness in its very walls. All you have to do is sit and let it seep in through your pores."

She opened her eyes and watched the countryside go by without really seeing it.

"The scent of the ocean is in everything, and whether you end up loving or hating it, you'll never leave feeling indifferent to it." She faced him again but this time without her earlier self-consciousness.

"My mother's mother left it to her, and her mother to her. Mother always laughed and said their menfolk never liked the place because it was so far away from civilisation, but I think that's why they loved it so. It was only there, in that special place, that we could be ourselves, without judgement."

"So I take it your father never stayed there with either of you?" He had leaned forward again, resting his forearms along the top of his thighs. His hair had fallen across one eye but he didn't appear to have noticed.

"Oh no. Father hates the sound of solitude. I'm not certain he would last a day with only his thoughts for company." Jane was grateful that her father hadn't ruined the cottage for her and her mother by insisting on being there with them. Of course, after her mother's death, he had put a stop to Jane going there altogether.

She shuddered to think what state it may have got into. If need be, she would see to any repairs herself. Her inheritance would see to that.

A sudden thought drew Jane to look away from Phillip: who would she leave the cottage to when she died? She would never have a daughter to pass it on to, or with whom to share the joy she and her own mother had discovered there.

Chapter Eight

That night, in his room at their inn in Southampton, Phillip threw the quilt back and sat on the edge of his bed. Even though the adjoining doors were closed between his and Jane's room, he could hear her pacing. Her room's wooden floor was clearly in need of attention, for it squeaked and creaked at her every step. It had reached a point where he was now hearing a strange music-like refrain from her pacing. He had already titled it *The Wedding Night Melody.*

Some wedding night, he thought: Jane locked in her room and he in his. Phillip had tried to remind himself of his promise, but every time he thought back to seeing Jane's entrance into her father's library before they'd left, resplendent in her plum-coloured lace dress, his mouth went dry and sleep slipped further and further from his reach. Of course, those thoughts had been before Jane's pacing had started. She must have waited until she thought he was asleep before beginning her incessant toing and froing. By now, he reckoned, she could have walked the rest of the way to her cottage. She had to be exhausted.

She was probably only just realising now how insane it was to believe they could carry this marriage off as he intended. Or better still, she was plotting a way to get him into her bed.

Phillip sighed and stood up. After their day travelling in close quarters, he almost wished she was indeed plotting to get him into her bed. He rubbed at his pounding head, trying to dislodge both that thought and his headache. Thy were foolish thoughts, of course. A weak man would never be able to carry off leaving his wife unbedded, certainly not if he continued thinking so much about how to keep it so. How, then, was he going to resist her soft sighs and curves? For one thing, he was going to have to stop his eyes from resting on the gentle outline of her breasts every time he thought she wasn't looking. He would also need to supress his need to gather her into his arms every time she inadvertently let the hurt her family had caused her show in her wonderful grey eyes—those eyes that changed with her every shifting mood and thought.

Jane's pacing finally stopped. Phillip made his way over to the connecting door and pressed his ear against it. Maybe she'd finally worn herself out and was now resting.

He was about to return to his bed when a knock came at the door. His heart leapt at the thought that maybe this was Jane beginning her seduction. Like some addled fool, he stood there for a few seconds wondering what to do. What if he opened the door and she was unclothed? Could he really deny her then? He wiped his hand across his dry mouth and sighed. Of course he couldn't.

With a feeling of dread and a smattering of hope he finally unlocked the door and turned the knob.

Phillip scolded his treacherous heart for being disappointed at seeing her fully clothed. Even her hair was combed back into a soft bun, pinned up at the nape of her neck.

Jane stepped a little way into his room, a quick glance around before settling her gaze upon him. "I know it's early, but I swear I can smell the sea from here and I can't sleep from wanting to be home in my cottage."

Phillip's heart dropped yet further. So she hadn't been pacing and plotting, merely wanting to be in her own home. In a way he envied her. Even though Greystone Hall had been in his family for more than eight generations, it had never felt like home to him. His mother had done the best she could to make it so, but it had been hard in the shadow of his father. Each night, once he'd begun drinking, he would always come looking for them. Over time, Phillip had taken to sleeping in the stables, his father normally too drunk to leave the house and hunt him down. Unfortunately, there had never been a place for his mother to hide.

Phillip ran a finger along the length of his scar, banishing his unbidden thoughts through concentrating on Jane. Some things could never be changed, so what point was there in dwelling on them?

"Just let me dress and wake the coachman," he said. "And I'll see if the landlord can arrange a basket of food for us to take along." He dearly wanted to reach out and touch her hair, just this once, just to know what it felt like.

"Oh. That's *too* much trouble, by far. I wouldn't want everyone disturbed like that." Jane looked more closely at his face. "And you look like you haven't had much rest yourself. Please, please forget I said anything."

She gently pushed his shoulder. "Go back to bed, and I will too."

It proved too tempting, and he had to reach out and run his fingers along the edge of her hairline. He had been right, it was soft. When she didn't pull back, he ran the same fingers along the edge of her chin. She hitched her breath, but never looked away, rooted in place.

Phillip finally came to his senses and stepped back, resolving that it was far too dangerous to be in the same room as his wife. She had a scent of lemons and fresh air, enough that he wanted nothing more than to bury his face into the curve of her neck, just to see if he could taste those very same scents.

He cleared his throat before hurrying to where his clothes were laid out for the following day's journey. "You need not worry, Jane; I pay our coachman a good enough wage."

Phillip grabbed his clothes and held them in front of himself, like some green schoolboy who had never been alone with a woman before.

"Go finish packing and I'll come and get you when everything's ready." Phillip didn't make a move to get dressed until Jane had closed the door behind her. Even then he had to sit on the edge of his bed and steady his heart before he could put his trousers on.

Chapter Nine

Jane told herself she was fanning her hot cheeks because the room was overly stuffy and her corset was cutting off her breath. Both of these things were the real reason she hadn't been able to sleep a wink all night and why she wanted to get the journey over with, but both palled into insignificance compared with the effect of being within mere inches of her new husband's bare chest.

Before retiring to her room she had been too embarrassed to ask Phillip if he would undo the many buttons of her dress and untie her corset so she could disrobe.

Phillip had obviously been so surprised by her midnight knock that he hadn't thought to grab his robe. Fortunately, or unfortunately, he'd still worn his breeches, even though they had been unbuttoned at the waist, revealing a muscled stomach that had made Jane's mouth go completely dry.

Well, at least she wouldn't die never having seen a man's bare chest and stomach. She might never discover what else a man covered so well beneath his breeches, but now she could think back to that perfect moment when she had stood chest to chest with

Phillip in the moonlight.

Jane closed her eyes and breathed in the inn's hot, stale air, but what actually filled her senses was how Phillip had smelled, so manly, of spice and something else that was so him. All she'd wanted to do as she'd stood before him in his room was touch his perfect chest. What would he have done had she done so?

To keep from dwelling on what could only bring her more pain, Jane stood and furiously rubbed at her wrinkled gown. She deeply regretted her restraint, for now she would never know how his chest would feel beneath her fingers. She had let the moment slip past because all she'd been able to hear whilst standing there had been the words of guidance her stepmother had offered moments before the wedding ceremony had taken place.

Jane suspected that advice had been more out of spite than concern. Her stepmother had laughed as she'd crudely explained the fundamentals of how a man and a woman came together for their nuptials, adding only that the whole thing was quite pleasant for the man but wholly painful for the woman. The she-devil had laughed at Jane's muddled expression, then had left her to replay those coarse facts over and over in her mind. But then what did it matter? It wasn't as though she was ever going to experience anything so personal with her own husband.

Fortunately, a rap came at the connecting door. She pulled at the high collar of her dress and took in as deep a breath as her corset would allow before going to open it.

"Solomon has the carriage ready. If your bags are packed, I'll send the innkeeper up for them and we'll be ready to leave." Phillip looked over her shoulder and into her room.

Jane didn't have the heart to tell him she'd not yet opened any of her bags. Without a lady's maid to help her undress, the only thing Jane had been able to do was wash those parts of her that she could reach, and comb her hair. She would have asked the innkeeper's wife to help, but the shame of having to admit she couldn't ask her own husband to unbutton her had been too great.

"Everything's already packed and ready to carry down." Before he could turn to go, Jane reached out and touched his arm. "When do you think we'll arrive in Weymouth?"

Phillip half turned to face her. "If we carry on right

through, not stopping to eat, then probably late after-noon. Would you like some tea before we leave?"

He searched her eyes until she shook her head, then he reached out and cupped her cheek with his hand. "You didn't touch your food at breakfast yester-day, and have only sipped a few drops of tea since we left your father's house. You're not unwell, are you?"

Heat rushed to Jane's face. It was his kind ex-pression that was her undoing. Tears filled her eyes both from her embarrassment and her discomfort. "I can't breathe. Lady Blackmore insisted on my corset being tightened even more than usual, saying she wanted me to look my best on my wedding day, but I know she had Harriet do it out of spite. When I asked if I could change my clothes before we left, she told me it was too late, that all my bags had been loaded and it was time for me to leave."

"Why didn't you ask for my help last night?" but before she could answer, he motioned her to turn around.

Jane crossed her arms in front of her chest before whispering, "What do you intend doing?"

"I'm going to help you out of this dress and corset. Do you have something more comfortable with you, or did your stepmother refuse you all your clothes?"

"Oh, no, she made certain I packed everything of mine. She said she didn't want to have a thing left in her house that would remind her of me."

When he turned her to face him, the tightening of a muscle in Phillip's jaw was the only indication that her words had had any effect on him.

"But...but you can't do this," she protested. "It wouldn't be proper, and the coachman and innkeeper are waiting on us," but he just waved towards her room.

"How is it not proper? We're husband and wife." When she didn't move, he gave her a gentle push and laughed at her pained expression. "If it helps to ease your mind, I promise not to look, all right?"

She nodded but couldn't meet his eyes, but then pointed towards the larger of her trunks. "My travelling dress is in that one. Maybe if you just unbutton my dress and unlace my corset I can do the rest."

But Phillip only turned her around and began unbuttoning her dress. With each button undone Jane could feel her breathing coming easier, until her back became exposed and his fingers brushed against her bare skin. She closed her eyes and tried her best to think about her cottage by the beach and running barefoot across the sand, but when he started untying her corset, her thoughts scattered and again she found it hard to breathe.

Jane's knees might well have buckled, but as Phillip finished, he slipped his arms around her waist and pulled her close against him. Too surprised to move, Jane allowed him to snuggle his face into the nape of her neck. He breathed in deeply, as if memorising her scent. They might have stood there forever in that sweet embrace had a knock not come from the hallway door.

Phillip released her and motioned for her to stay there before he went and unlocked the door and opened it a crack. He peered out.

A deep voice asked, "Your Grace, are you ready for your baggage to be taken down to your carriage?"

If Jane wasn't already discomfited enough, her knowing that there were people waiting simply because she had wanted to leave in the middle of the night only added more heat to her already burning cheeks. Because of her, people were losing their sleep, and now they would have to wait upon her changing her clothes. She should never have mentioned her discomfort to Phillip. Had she kept silent they would now be on their way, the innkeeper and his servants soon back in the comforts of their own beds.

"I realise this must be a bit of an imposition," Phillip was now saying to the innkeeper, "but if you wouldn't mind waiting a little longer. We will be with you shortly."

When Phillip shut the door and turned to face her, Jane asked, "If you'd unlatch my trunk, I'll get out of this dress."

For a moment he just stood there, grinning, then quietly said, "However topsy-turvy this night is turning out to be, at least it has brought me sight of my striking wife's most lovely naked back. I think our second day of marriage is going quite beautifully, don't you?"

Jane dropped her dress to the floor around her ankles, taking great pleasure from his surprised look, and the glint of something else that quickly surfaced in his eyes.

Chapter Ten

The carriage rocked over every bump, and with each Jane was thrown ever closer to Phillip. Exhaustion had won over early in the journey, and after several attempts at staying awake, Jane had fallen into such a deep sleep that even if a band of highway robbers had stopped the coach it seemed she might have very well slept through it all.

Seeing such exhaustion convinced Phillip she hadn't managed one good night's sleep since the night of the ball.

The thought of Jane trying to hide behind those potted ferns made him smile. Phillip had never given such plants much thought, but since that night they had found a special place in his heart—those and the colour yellow. Both had set his life onto a different course. No longer was he so certain of his convictions.

For the first part of the journey Phillip had remained seated on his side of their carriage, but seeing Jane being almost thrown from the seat at times, he had moved next to her, wrapping his arm around her shoulders to keep her safe. Well, at least that was what he had told himself.

Just this once, Phillip wanted what he knew he

could not have—not and still keep his promise. With his nose buried in Jane's dark mane, though, he began to question the worth of such a promise. How could any child of Jane's ever be anything other than perfect? Maybe whatever it was that passed from father to son would not pass from him to a son of theirs, and would finally stop at him.

Phillip rested his head on top of Jane's and closed his eyes. Unfortunately, her scent of lemon brought back the memory of seeing her in her room at the inn, her dress pooled around her ankles. He forced himself to open his eyes and draw his face from against her hair, staring resolutely out of the window. As a distraction, he made a list in his mind of all those things he needed to do before he could safely leave Jane in the cottage by the sea, before he could return to Greystone Hall. His concentration soon flagged, his thoughts once more drifting back to Jane's slender form.

He had been bewitched by her look of innocence, but unsure of her seeming invitation, one he convinced himself she'd been unaware of making. It had been her look of hurt, though, when he'd busied himself finding her traveling dress, that had cut the deepest. She would never know just how hard it had been for him to resist removing her remaining garments, so he could then have feasted his eyes on her perfect body. Even as he had buttoned her into her traveling dress he had longed to slip it back off and immerse himself in his beautiful wife. Had he done so, he'd argued then, just that once, they would then truly have been married in more than just name. With great difficulty, he had stayed resolute enough for cold reason to tell him that with Jane it could only ever be all or nothing.

Somehow, he was going to have to remain resistant to his lovely bride. Phillip wasn't certain how long his resolve could last and so knew he had to make all arrangements for Jane's needs at the cottage without delay, in preparation for his protracted absences. He could then return to his own growing problems at Greystone Hall, secure in the knowledge that Jane would be well taken care of. Then he could try to forget he even had a wife.

Jane stirred in his arms and his stomach felt heavy, as though weighed down by stones. He suspected it would take more than the distance of miles ever to forget that Jane was now his. Despite himself, that thought brought a smile to his lips—the thought that she was now his very own.

Chapter Eleven

Jane almost cried when she awoke only to discover she had been dreaming a wonderful dream. In it she had been safe in Phillip's arms, but there he now was on the seat opposite her in their carriage, looking out of the window as though she wasn't even here. Was he going to spend the rest of their journey avoiding her eyes?

Was she quite so hideous? She must be, she decided, having seen how he'd occupied himself removing her blue muslin dress from her trunk and determinedly dressing her. The memory brought a crimson blush from her neck to the top of her head.

She hadn't planned on seducing him. It had just seemed to happen, however clumsily, but it had come to naught. He'd fumbled with her buttons in his haste to return her her modesty and to get them away from the inn, as though he feared she would reveal more.

Jane covered her eyes, vainly trying to block out the memory of Phillip's shocked face—no, his look of horror. So she really would remain a virgin, and all alone.

She could have kept her face covered for the remainder of the journey, only the sound of seagulls to keep her company, but the view through the window eventually drew her to look out. She was surprised to see a scattering of cottages, and although it had been more than ten years since her last visit to Weymouth, she still recognised them.

"Do you feel any better now you've had some sleep?" Phillip's asked, as though but a courtesy.

Jane absently reached up to check her hair bun was still pinned in place. "I still have a little bit of my headache, but at least I can breathe now. Thank you for that." She determined that she would refuse to spend the rest of her life afraid of speaking her mind, especially to the man who was now her husband.

He, though, only looked out of the window. "We should be arriving in Weymouth soon. Is your cottage far from the town?"

His mention of the cottage had Jane almost leaning out of the window. "It's about five miles out on the other side of Weymouth."

She couldn't help but turn to Phillip with an excited look beaming from her face. "I can't wait to see the sea again. As you know, Father refused to let me visit after Mother's death. He said it would only hold bad memories for me, but I knew how much he hated the coast. He said he could never get the sand out of his boots after the one time he did come down here."

Phillip slid forward in his seat, their knees now touching, which drew her attention away from the passing countryside and back onto him. He cleared his throat and a blush crept into his cheeks. "I'm sorry I didn't think about engaging a lady's maid to accompany you on the journey." He pulled at his collar. "I'm new to all this, Jane, to matrimony, but I trust you will speak up if I do something wrong or am remiss in any way. I should have thought that you would have needed help with your toilette."

Jane patted his hand. "Such a thing is the lady's responsibility, Phillip. My stepmother surprised me by offering her own lady's maid—just for the journey and until I might find a maid of my own in Weymouth, you understand. But I wanted nothing of that woman, nothing. So I demurred, and will look to engage someone in Weymouth myself. In the meantime, I'm prepared to suffer the inconvenience. So, if anyone's at fault, it is myself alone."

He inched nearer, his leg sliding a little way beside her own. "But her offer would have made things so much easier for you, Jane, and would have avoided last night's—"

"But don't you see, Phillip, if I had accepted, my

stepmother would then have had a spy in our midst, one I would have been paying for. Would you really wish news of our own affairs winging their way back to her?"

She looked out of the window and swallowed. "How long would it be before my father demanded proof that our marriage has been consummated?"

She met his eyes again. "My stepmother hates me, and once she becomes bored with her new life, she's going to need another way to venture a vendetta against me."

Phillip reached over and took her hand. "I had no idea her hatred of you ran so deep. Why does she despise you so?"

"I lived where none of her own babies did. She sees me as living proof that she's failed my father as a wife. She wanted to give him a son, to gain his greater esteem and to provide him with an heir. Do you now see?"

"I do, and so I'm glad you're out of her house for good, away from her malign control."

He looked away, but then added. "I may not be the husband you wanted, but I'll never wish you harm."

He finally met her eyes again. "Rest assured that

I'll come back and be here for you, any time you need my help. However else I may let you down, content yourself that you will always be in my thoughts."

Chapter Twelve

If Phillip lived to be a hundred, he would never forget the look on Jane's face when the carriage finally drew to a halt outside her cottage. Her eyes widened like saucers and she seemed afraid to blink. She jumped down without waiting for him or the coachman to help her out, and then ran as fast as her long skirts would allow to its front door. He had no idea any woman could run that fast or with such purpose.

It wasn't until she'd begun opening the door that she turned to look back at him. "Come on. You walk like an old man," but she softened the insult by softly smiling. "I hope it hasn't gone to rack and ruin because of father's neglect." She stepped in but then stopped and turned her startled face to him.

Phillip hadn't realised he'd been holding his breathe until he saw her bright smile lighting up her face. She took his hand and pulled him inside.

A fire had been lit in the front room but all the windows facing out onto a small garden and the beach beyond were open. Their white lace curtains were blowing in the sea breeze and a wonderful smell of baking wafted through the sunlit house. He could see why Jane loved her cottage. He too had felt its welcome the moment he'd entered. The overstuffed couch and chairs may have been a little worn but they still looked inviting.

Jane ran from object to object about the room, holding some to her chest as if relieved to see they still existed, each one caressed before being set back in its appointed place. She finally turned back to him. "It hasn't changed a bit since the last time I was here, as though Mother had never left. And everything looks so well cared for. How can that be so?"

Before Phillip could answer a sturdy looking elderly lady breezed in through one of the doors to the room. Her grey hair was tied back, a single ribbon holding it in place, although a few strands had come lose and were awry about her kindly-looking face.

"My word," she exclaimed. "You gave me such a fright, Your Grace, and My Lady. I wasn't expecting you until later tonight. You must have made good time."

The old housekeeper wiped her hands on her apron as she looked at Phillip, but then she turned to Jane and her face lit up. "My, my, but you're the spitting image of your mother, Ma'am. Even as a child you had the look of her about you."

Jane placed the gold-framed picture she'd been

holding back on its table and gazed at the woman. Finally, with a small gasp, she said, "Helen? Is it really you?" then she rushed across the room and threw her arms around her, kissing her cheeks and laughing. "I can't believe you're still here. No wonder the place looks so spick and span. You always took such good care of mother and me."

"Your mother requested in her will that Silas and I keep the place in good repair, Ma'am. There isn't a day we're aren't here, keeping everything in order." She waved toward the fireplace. "I've always kept embers going in case you were ever to surprise us with a visit, but I would hazard your father has never allowed it." She sniffed. "I must say: I'm not surprised. He hated this place and the time it took your mother away from him, but she did love it so."

The housekeeper then addressed Phillip. "You don't know how pleased we were to hear you had married, Sir."

Jane was shocked to realise she'd forgotten Phillip. "Helen, this is my husband, Phillip Radcliff, The Duke of Greystone. Phillip, this is Helen. She bakes the best teacakes in the world. They all but melt in your mouth." Jane closed her eyes, as if the memory had to be savoured in private, and a smile tugged at her lips.

Phillip offered the housekeeper his hand. "I know it's an unusual request, but I hope you won't feel uncomfortable calling me Phillip." He glanced around the room. "I think it only fitting, for this place does seem to lend itself to a rare intimacy I'm not certain the rest of the world would understand."

When Helen tentatively offered her own hand into his still outstretched one, he surprised her greatly when he bent and kissed it. The housekeeper immediately turned as red as a beetroot and her mouth dropped open. "I don't know what to say, Sir," she stuttered. "I've never been called upon to address a duke by his given name before. I'm all a fluster. Even here, Sir, it doesn't seem right."

Phillip released Helen's hand, a wide smile across his face. "But in this house Jane makes the rules." He turned to her. "So, what do you say, Jane? Are we allowed to break a few rules here, in this secluded domain?"

Jane grinned. "But I think that's a wonderful idea, Phillip. It's about time we shunned the very people who have worked so tirelessly to shun us. Why should we give a fig for society here?"

She leaned in and whispered, "I should warn you

in advance, I never wear shoes whilst I'm here. I hope it doesn't shock you when I forgo stockings and shoes." She grinned even wider at his surprise. "Well, you did say we could break a few rules, and you never know, I might like to try my hand at breaking them all, in time."

Phillip swallowed past a lump in his throat at the mischievous look on Jane's face. He really was going to have to leave soon for Greystone Hall or he might end up breaking a few of his own rules if Jane continued to look so happy and carefree. At least one of them was going to have their heart's desire, but he had a terrible feeling that if he left, it was going to be him who missed out on one he'd never known until now he had ever wanted.

Chapter Thirteen

Jane poured more tea into hers and Phillip's cups before taking another slice of cake and putting it onto her rose-patterned plate. She didn't care that it was her third piece or that Phillip was now grinning from ear to ear.

It wasn't until she'd sat in the very chair she and her mother used to share that she'd realised just how starving she felt. So what did it matter if her new husband thought she was making a pig of herself? for that was the clear intention of the look he'd just given her. She was going to enjoy her tea and cake, and if she did get as large as a house, who was there here to care? Her husband clearly didn't. Any man who could set eyes on her almost naked body and act as though he hadn't noticed would hardly be concerned about how large she may become.

"You're right. This cake does melt in the mouth," he said, inadvertently spitting out a few crumbs with his last laughed words.

"Do you not think it unseemly to make fun of someone you've just barely met." She grinned in spite of trying to look offended.

He took another bite. "Doesn't it count for something that I've already seen you in your pantaloons?"

Jane's mouth dropped open and she glance at the door leading to the kitchen. "Shush."

"Ah, so we're back to that, are we? Isn't that what got us into this trouble in the first place? Your shushing me," he chastised, his grin softening the question.

Jane lifted her nose and shifted in her seat. "I did tell you to leave, if you remember. Is it my fault you didn't listen?"

He took another bite. "But look what I would have missed, otherwise. I'm in a lovely house in an even lovelier setting and with an even lovelier woman, so it strikes me that my not leaving you alone was one of the most sensible things I've ever done."

A warmth spread through Jane, everything around her seeming a little brighter and even more welcoming then before. She lowered her lashes and took another bite of her cake, for how exactly did one respond to the sweetest thing ever said to one? She tried not to smile but her lips refused her and curved of their own free will.

She cleared her throat. "More tea?" and met his smiling eyes as he nodded, then she poured the tea as though her heart wasn't in her throat.

As Phillip accepted his cup, he asked, "So when do I get the grand tour? I can't wait to see the rest of the place I've seen you travel to every time you close your eyes."

Jane's mouth popped open. "How did you know?"

He glanced around the room. "After entering this house, how could I not? It's charming. I felt its warmth the moment I came in through its front door. It feels like somewhere that has only ever known love." He looked back at her. "I wish I had had such a wonderful place to run off to every time my life became too much to bear."

Had it not been so unseemly for a lady, Jane would have jumped up and kissed her new husband. For the first time since her mother's death, she now felt understood. She hadn't realised before just how bereft she'd felt, not having someone who really knew her, but Phillip had voiced what her heart had known for a long time. But, of course, he was only being kind, although if friendship was all she could offer, then she would chose that in place of being his real wife.

"Well, now you do. My home is now your home, so why shouldn't you run off here whenever you need to." She smiled, hoping she'd sounded as sincere as her words had been meant.

He stood and pulled her to her feet. "We're wasting the daylight. I want to see everything."

Standing chest to chest against Phillip made Jane's mouth go dry. To think of anything but what his lips might feel like pressed to hers, she looked down at his feet. "But first, you'll have to take off your boots."

He laughed. "You think me too boorish not to enjoy a little sand between my toes?"

She sat back down and removed her slippers. "Of course not, but I do think you should turn around, because I'd hate to shock you when I take off my stockings."

To her surprise, Phillip knelt at her feet. "But my dear wife, I thought I was to be your lady's maid until we engage one for you, so isn't helping you remove your stockings one of my new duties?" He placed his hands around one of her calves before she could reply, but then looked up at her before lifting the skirt of her dress.

Jane cursed that third slice of cake, so uneasily did it now rest in her stomach. Never in her life had a man ever placed his hand upon her leg, the intimacy sending such tremors of shock through her that she felt unsettled, unable to choose which sensation to acknowledge: her unsettled stomach, her erratic heartbeat or a completely new urge that seemed to pool within her loins.

Before she knew it, her own hands were helping lift her skirt, her mind clinging to the little control it seemed to offer. But then she looked away when his fingers slid higher. The act struck her as far too intimate for a man determined to keep his distance, but she did not protest, only savoured the moment. She could imagine this being her new place to which to retreat when in future she closed her eyes, and the thing she would then long for next—a husband who really did love her.

Chapter Fourteen

It was nearing sunset but still Phillip and Jane walked along the shoreline below the cliffs of her cottage. The water was by now lapping across their feet and Jane had to raise her skirts so they wouldn't become any wetter than they already were.

Phillip glanced over to see if she was getting chilled, whether he should suggest they go back to the cottage, but her eyes never wavered from staring out across the water. It was fascinating to see how different she seemed, now she was where she had so longed to be. It was like she was afraid to blink, in case it all went away.

After a few more moments of his own staring, Jane finally turned to look at him. "You must be ready to go back. Mother always used to say that I never knew when to go home once I'd started walking out here." A light breeze stirred her hair away from her forehead, revealing an even more beautiful face. "It's just so peaceful. Here, I can pretend that the rest of the world just doesn't exist."

She smiled and shrugged. "I know how silly that sounds, but isn't it nice to have such a place to escape to every now and then, when the world gets too much to bear?"

Phillip nodded, although what he really wanted to do was pull her close against his chest and kiss her. How easy it would be, here in this peaceful place, to forget his problems and fall in love with his wife.

Why not turn Greystone Hall and its worries over to his first cousin, Reuben? The man was certainly haughty enough to fill the position. While he and Reuben had never been fond of each other as children, his cousin understood the Greystone estate and would certainly keep it going. But what would Phillip's mother say about such a change? Would she be upset to have to move out of Greystone Hall or relieved to be away from all its bad memories?

"You're thinking much too hard for this setting. Seeing your worry lines tells me it must be time to return to the real world." Jane then smiled and reached over to take his hand.

Phillip squeezed her fingers. "I didn't mean to ruin your walk. Let's do this again, in the morning, and I promise to leave all my troubles behind."

They turned for the path up to the cottage, now more hurried, then Jane glanced at Phillip. "I know this marriage was something neither you or I wanted, but I refuse to be sad about it."

She paused, clearly thinking, then went on: "No. I can't be sad, because you're so kind, and I don't believe that even if I searched into old age, I'd ever find a better man for a husband." She came to a halt, and so did Phillip. "I know you can't stay, but maybe you could linger a few days longer, so we can get to know each that little bit better. I would hate to think I never knew your likes and dislikes. Shouldn't a good wife know such things?"

Phillip brushed the hair from her forehead and kissed her brow. "I think I can spare my wife a few days more." How he longed to do more than kiss her forehead, all the time chiding himself for being so weak, too weak to keep just one promise.

He would never be the husband Jane deserved, he knew that. Even now he could feel the drink calling to him. It always did this when his thoughts tarried too long on the past. He was afraid one day that its call would be too strong to resist and he would then turn into his father. Phillip couldn't bear the thought of ever hurting Jane, as his father had done to his mother. It was better the cycle stopped with him, even if it meant he would have to stay at Greystone Hall and Jane here. At least she was happy in this place, and knowing that would have to be enough for him.

He noticed Jane shiver and so drew her closer, wrapping his arms around her waist. He told himself it was to keep her warm, that it had nothing to do with his yearning, one that grew stronger the longer they were together.

Chapter Fifteen

The sound of the surf and the warmth of the rocks seeping through the fabric of her dress had Jane nearly dozing, which she might have done had Phillip not been repeatedly tracing his finger down the length of her arm.

The previous seven days would had been just perfect, if not for the knowledge that it would soon come to an end. Just that morning she had heard Phillip telling Solomon to drive into the village to get the supplies he needed for his return journey.

But maybe it was better if he did leave now, before she did something stupid, like dropping her gown to the floor again—not that it had worked the first time. He seemed completely immune to her charms. She often caught him staring whenever he thought she wasn't looking, and even now, when he should be napping, he was touching her. He was always touching her.

As Jane had no experience in matters of love, she feared she might be wrong about Phillip desiring her. But it would be wonderful if he did. Maybe he only intended returning to Greystone Hall to conclude some business before returning. During his time with her here, he'd steadily lost most of that haunted look he gained whenever his thoughts drifted away. She wondered where they did indeed drift away to.

Phillip's tantalising touch began to tickle and Jane giggled. Then, without opening her eyes, she said, "Has it ever occurred to you that I might eat your teacakes when you aren't looking, as well as my own?"

Feeling his breath hot on her cheek, Jane opened her eyes and discovered him leaning over her. It was the perfect moment for a kiss. It would have been natural to do so, but she didn't, for she remembered her promise, that she would remain his friend and not force him into anything more. She wanted him to come to her without enticement, simply because he could not live without her. Besides, it would certainly be easier to watch him leave if they had no regret hanging over them for an ill-conceived intimacy. Even in her inexperience in such matters, she could see he was struggling to keep his distance, but then why was he making it so much harder on himself by for ever touching her? On her part, though, it only made her want more than she knew she could have.

"I'm not at all worried," Phillip at last answered. "Helen has learned your evil ways. She always hides more cakes for me in the kitchen." He kissed the end of her nose before standing and offering her his hand.

"Do we have to go back so soon?" Jane said as she reluctantly took his hand, a last longing look cast briefly at the gently rolling waves crashing softly onto the beach.

"You would stay out here all day if you had your way." He patted his flat stomach. "I for one am starving. Surely you can spare a few minutes for us to enjoy our lunch."

Phillip helped Jane down from the rocks, where she then enjoyed standing close up against his chest. Soon enough, he would leave, so why waste such a good opportunity to feel his heart beating against her breast?

Jane feared he might step back, but instead he tucked a strand of her hair behind her ear. "When I leave, I'll miss you more than you'll ever know."

Jane reached up and placed her hands flat against his chest and searched his face. "I'll not ask you to stay if you feel you must return home. But I can't let you leave without telling you: you've become very dear to me. If you could find it within you to stay, I would...would like that very much."

Phillip pulled her closer and whispered, "It's so

tempting to forget my oath, but over the last few days I've only told you my happy childhood memories. They are few and far between, but I didn't want to ruin our time together here by telling you the worst."

His gaze wandered from her eyes and out toward the sea. "My mother and I lived through hell, and even now, here in this place, I can feel the devil that made my father what he was, such a monster—the siren call of spirits. In my wilder days I too followed his path, unknowingly, falling into the bottle, but fortunately, before it was too late, I realised I was becoming him, becoming the monster that was my father. And so I swore I would never touch another drop."

Phillip met her gaze again. "I have no wish to be that monster. More importantly, I refuse to put you through what my mother had to endure. What would happen to us, my dear Jane, if I were to give in, to fall once again into the brandy and whisky bottle?"

He drew her face close to his. "I would much prefer leaving here as your friend than one day waking up to see only hate in your eyes."

Jane wrapped her arms around him. "I don't think you have it in you ever to hurt anyone."

He pressed his lips against her temple. "I wish I was who you believe me to be, but I'm more damaged than you'll ever know. Every so often I feel that same rage I saw in my father's face, when he hunted us both down, murder in his eyes. Fortunate it was that we learnt to recognise it before it consumed him, for I think neither of us would then have been alive today."

He stepped back and averted his eyes. "The day my father died, the rage from all my years of fear and pain, that I'd tried bottled up, burst forth and blinded me. Blinded me to all but the demon in my father's face that I then saw in myself."

Phillip ran his finger along his scar, then stared straight into her eyes. "I wish I could know for certain that I would never become my father, for then I could move on, could be the husband you truly deserve."

Jane reached out and took his hand. She couldn't bear to see how much pain he was in. "I refuse to believe you could ever be anything other than an honourable man. Maybe it's time to let the past go and concentrate on our future."

"Do you think I could?" and he pulled her tighter against himself.

"I think you can do anything—if you want to hard enough." To keep him there, Jane wrapped her arms around his waist and threaded her fingers together.

Phillip pressed into her. "You have no idea how

much I want to believe such a thing were possible."

Jane stood on her tiptoes. "Then kiss me and we'll find out together."

In one fluid move Phillip lifted her off the ground and into his arms.

"I don't know what I ever did to deserve someone as sweet as you, but I thank all the stars in the heavens that you picked my corner of the ballroom in which to hide away."

Jane pushed his hair out of his eyes and nodded toward the path that led to their cottage. It seemed a distance too far when all she now wanted to do was kiss her new husband.

"Surely you don't intend carrying me all the way back to the cottage."

His now wicked grin sent a rush of heat through her, and all she could do was bury her face into the curve of his neck, only meeting his eyes again once he'd knelt and lowered her softly onto the sand.

He knelt before her, his eyes drinking her in. "I'm going to kiss you now," and all she could do was nod.

His hand slipped through her hair to rest firmly behind her head as he leaned forward towards her upturned mouth. But when he trailed a kiss down the side of her face and onto her neck, Jane wrapped her arms around him and drew him down as she lay back on the sand. Only then, their bodies pressed tightly together, did she let her every concern be carried away on the breeze that gently blew along the shore. Now there seemed to be too many layers of fabric between them, between her and her husband, and so, like a good wife, she began to remove them.

Chapter Sixteen

Four months and twenty-four days—Jane sighed and tried to stop counting how long it had been since seeing Phillip, but each passing day only confirmed the two things she was growing more certain about. Phillip wasn't coming back and she was carrying his child.

Jane closed her eyes against the one thing that usually brought her happiness—the sea, but how could it do so now her heart was breaking? For two perfect weeks she and Phillip had found such joy here, and during that short time Jane had thought they were going to be happy together for ever. Even after she'd woken up to a brief note from him, saying he'd be back soon, Jane hadn't worried until the days had rolled into months and not even a letter had arrived.

An overwhelming wave of sadness brought Jane's knees to buckle, forcing her to sit on a nearby rock. To keep from losing her breakfast, she lowered her head between her knees and drew in deep breaths, until she finally raised her head again and concentrated on the incoming waves.

She rubbed at her stomach. "If it is only going to

be the two of us, I will see to it that you only know joy. That's all this place has ever known. I refuse to be the one to change that now."

She heard her name and lifted her head, gazing toward the pathway that led to the cottage, a little alarmed at the sight of Silas quickly making his way through the soft sand toward her.

"Mistress!" he called and waved, and Jane stood and hurried to meet him.

"Whatever is the matter, Silas? Has something happened to Helen?" Jane had never seen him like this before. He'd always been so calm. But the sight of him now disquieted her.

Jane tried to be patient as the man caught his breath, a whole litany of catastrophes running through her mind. "Silas, whatever has happened to put you into such a state?"

"The duke and duchess are here, demanding to see you at once, Ma'am. The duke was most insistent you attend him without delay."

Her father and stepmother were here? That didn't bode well. Her stepmother never did anything without some foul motive.

Jane patted Silas's shoulder. "Take your time. I'll not see you having a heart attack on my account."

"But the duke was most adamant, Ma'am, He even sent me to find you before he'd have his horses stabled." Silas drew in another deep breath that did nothing to improve his colour.

Jane rested her hands on her hips. "You are not my father's retainer but mine, so you answer to me, Silas. Besides, his coachman should be the one to take care of such things." She patted Silas's arm again. "Now do as I say and rest. I'll see what my father wants and how quickly I can send him on his way."

Jane's bravado lasted until she reached the footpath and then worry set in. What did this visit mean? She looked heavenward and pleaded it not be bad news about Phillip. Could this be why she hadn't received word back from him? and that terrible thought followed her all the way back to the cottage. When she finally and quietly entered the parlour, it was with a disquieted mind. She had hoped never to witness her father and stepmother breeching the sanctity of her home, but there they were: her stepmother busy barking orders at Helen, her father chatting with a stranger. Neither noticed her arrival.

She calmly settled herself before speaking out.

"Father, this is an unexpected pleasure," and she almost choked at her own insincerity.

Though they hadn't seen each other since the day of her marriage, the duke didn't rush to her. She'd not expected any sign of his affection, but a small part of her heart still desired it. Her dreams of ever having a devoted father had long since withered on the vine, and she knew better of her stepmother. The time for wishing had now long passed.

Stratton Blackmore crossed his arms. "I didn't know I needed an invitation to my own daughter's home."

Jane positioned herself behind the settee, gripping its back to steady her nerves. "Of course not, Father, but if you had, I could then have asked Helen to prepare a meal in honour of your arrival."

"There's no need for that. Your mother and I only came to take you home." He glanced at his wife, as though seeking her approval.

Before Jane could recover from her shock, the duchess informed her, "I was just telling Helen to prepare some food for our return journey. Your father and I had thought to rest a night here before returning, but," and she sniffed, "that was before I realised the place you were forever going on and on about is nothing more than a hovel, one not fit for man nor beast." She sniffed again and gave Jane a look that made her want to strike the woman sharply across her face.

Jane met Helen's eyes, the poor, sweet-natured women clearly distraught at being so powerless.

Jane straightened her spine. "But why would I need to go back with you? My understanding is that this cottage and its surrounding property were included in mine and Phillip's marriage contract."

Stratton Blackmore lifted his chin, making him appear even haughtier than he usually did. "Which I've instructed my lawyer to look into breaking, as soon as we've returned to London."

"That cannot be legal?" She swallowed past a lump that had formed in her throat and gripped the settee even harder. Where was Phillip when she so dearly needed him?

Duke Rutherford turned to the stranger beside him. "This gentleman is my personal physician. I've brought him here to examine you. It's come to our attention that your husband has abandoned you here. And so, given you've had no chance to consummate your marriage, it can be annulled."

Jane smiled for the first time since their arrival.

"I'm sorry, Father, but you're going to have to leave here sorely disappointed."

She turned a mischievous grin towards her stepmother. "And just so you know, it doesn't hurt at all. In fact, my husband's every touch brought me only pleasure, so you can take your hate with you as you go home."

A furious blush coloured Lady Blackmore's face. "You really are a common whore, aren't you?"

Jane laughed. "If loving my husband makes me a whore, then yes, I most certainly am." She motioned to her father's physician. "Let's get this over with and then you can leave my house, never to set foot in it again. Then," and she turned to her father, a sick feeling settling in her stomach, "you can do what you do best, Father, pretend I don't exist."

Chapter Seventeen

The sun peeked out from behind the clouds for the first time that morning but Jane barely noticed, so busy was she running ahead of the waves. It was a game her mother had invented years before, as something to help her expend her excess energies. To keep her worries at bay she had taken it up again, busy pretending to be five once more. It meant she didn't see the approaching figure until the older woman was nearly upon her.

Jane glanced up from her silly game only to stop dead in her tracks. In her shock she let go of her skirts and didn't notice when the water swilled around her feet, wetting their hems.

Was that really Phillip's mother? her skirts gathered almost around her waist, her feet as bare as the day she was born. What would society have to say if they'd seen the two of them out here on the beach with so little regard for propriety? The sight would certainly have caused a scandal, one that would have kept tongues wagging for weeks.

The thought made Jane chuckled, a smile still on her face when her mother-in-law reached her.

"It does my heart good to see that marriage to my

son agrees with you." The dowager patted Jane's cheek. "I was afraid that in my Phillip's absence you would be withering away, but your face is fuller now than the day you were married."

Jane took her hand. "Is Phillip well?" Her heart skipped a beat whilst she waited for an answer.

The older woman now patted Jane's hand. "As far as I know."

"What do you mean? Is he not at Greystone Hall?" Jane pulled her mother-in-law away from the waves that were again dragging at their skirts. She led her to an outcrop of rocks and insisted the dowager sit down.

The woman lifted the hem of her dress and rung the water from it, then looked up from her task. "I thought you might at least have had a letter from him," she softly said, "but I can see from your worried expression that you know as little as I do."

She dropped her skirt and patted the spot beside her. "You look faint. Sit before you fall down. I wouldn't want you harming yourself...or the baby."

Jane's mouth dropped open, but then she just as quickly ground her teeth together in anger. "Don't tell me. My stepmother has been blabbing."

She sat next to the dowager. "What rumours is

she spreading? Go on, I can take whatever it is." Jane closed her eyes and drew in a deep breath.

Her mother-in-law reached over and took Jane's hand. "I'm sure no one believes it."

Jane opened her eyes and met hers, a feeling of sickness washing over her. "Please, what has she said?"

"The duchess is telling everyone that she and your father came out here for a visit, to see how you were faring in your new life, but instead of finding you with Phillip, you were here with another man. When your father asked you to return home with them, you bragged of being pregnant by this other man. She's told everyone that that's why Phillip has left you here, why he isn't having anything to do with you."

Jane bent over and hung her head between her knees, shame and bitterness washing over her. For a brief moment, she contemplated walking out into the waves and letting them drag her under, but then her unborn baby kicked and she remembered what was truly important to her.

What did it matter out here what society thought of her? But where was her Phillip? If he really loved her, surely he wouldn't have left in the first place, nor stayed away as he had.

Jane finally sat back and lifted her eyes to the dowager. "It's not true, but then when has truth ever mattered?" She swept her dark mane out of her eyes and looked out at the rolling waves. Here was where her heart lay, where she was closest to the only person who had ever loved her—her mother. Let the rest of the world believe what it will. In a few months' time they will have forgotten she'd ever existed, and she would have her own child to love. No one could take that away from her, so let them talk.

'We both know the duchess is lying, so what do we do about it?" The dowager squeezed Jane's fingers and waited.

Jane stood. "Let's get out of these wet clothes and ask Helen to make us tea."

She slipped her arm through her mother-in-law's. "You must be exhausted and hungry. She's a wonderful cook."

On their way toward the path the dowager said, "I want you to go back to Greystone Hall with me. I've been thinking about throwing a party to celebrate yours and Phillip's wedding."

"Before I will agree to anything, though, you must tell me everything you know. For example, why you don't know Phillip's whereabouts. I thought he had gone back to Greystone Hall." Jane wrapped a handful of her skirt in one hand and let the warmth of the sand beneath her feet lend her some comfort as she wondered what could have befallen him.

Her mother-in-law nodded. "Philip did come home, but only briefly."

She came to a halt and faced Jane, taking both her hands in hers. "The look on his face when he arrived," and she smiled wistfully, then raised Jane's hands to her lips and kissed her fingers. "I've never seen my son so happy. If I didn't love you before, I did the moment I saw his face and how happy you had clearly made him."

"But if he was so happy, why has he stayed away?"

"The only reason he came back to Greystone Hall was to ask me if I would mind him relinquishing his title to his cousin, Reuben."

The dowager slipped her arm through Jane's and urged them on. "I told him that nothing would make me happier than to see him contented. My sister has been begging me to move in with her and her family for years. I only stayed at Greystone Hall after my husband's death so Phillip wouldn't have to face living there all by himself. I know how many bad memories he has of that place, as we both do." She patted Jane's hand again. "So, of course I want him to do what's best for himself...and for you."

"So I don't understand why you don't know where he is now?" Jane stopped them once more and waited.

"We can't get in contact with his cousin. It's as though he's dropped from the face of the Earth. So, when Phillip grew tired of sending him letters that were never answered, he went off to find him in person."

Jane nodded. "But what has any of this to do with me going to Greystone Hall with you? Wouldn't Phillip want me to stay here and just wait for his return?"

"I'm sure that's what he planned but your stepmother has changed all that. We can't let her ruin your or my grandchild's name. You're going to come back with me and show everyone that you're not hiding here because my son doesn't want you. Somehow, I'm going to find out where Phillip is and insist he come back home. We're going to throw an outlandish party and show everyone that your stepmother is nothing more than a barefaced liar."

Chapter Eighteen

Every turn of the carriage's wheels took Jane further and further from home. In truth she was overjoyed to be seeing Phillip again, although not as certain as the dowager appeared to be—now sitting opposite and beside the much-too-handsome Viscount Robert Worthington—that he would be happy to see her. Surely, if he missed her at all, he would have found a way to get at least one letter to her since leaving.

In spite of the chilly air, heat rushed to Jane's cheeks as she recalled their last night together. For two short weeks she had had everything a woman could want, a man who had, by every sign, cherished her. During the daytime he had wanted to know her every thought, and at night... Jane closed her eyes and savoured the thought that Phillip had given her fourteen nights of pure pleasure.

She sighed as she remembered them in their bed, his touching, his teaching, and his delving into her soul. And then, after he'd stolen her heart, he'd left with only a brief note to explain himself, lying there on the spot where his head should have lain.

Jane had no idea she could feel even more bereft

than she had before Phillip had come into her life, but seeing that note had stolen her breathe away and shattered her heart. Even though it had said he would return, she had eventually lost all hope. Now she was to face him again, she prayed he would never know that for a little while at least she had doubted his whispered words of love. But how could she not have, having spent so many years with people who cared nothing for her?

Every day of Phillip's absence, she had closed her eyes and sought the memory of his face. She no longer looked for happiness at her cottage, now she remembered her husband and what they had meant to each, or at least what he had meant to her—everything.

Jane turned from watching the endless trees pass by and regarded the presently fast asleep Viscount Robert Worthington. How was it possible that, after travelling for five days down the length of the country to Jane's cottage in the company of the dowager, and the equal duress of their return journey to Derbyshire, Phillip's friend still looked so dashing and so composed?

This was only Jane's fifth day and she felt grubby from all the dust, and her every joint ached. She was

117

sorely tempted to slip her hand to her hip and back, to massage them both. The dowager and the viscount both had their eyes closed but it would have been just her luck for them to open them just as she was rubbing her now numb derriere.

The viscount stirred, and so Jane turned her gaze back to the passing view. That day the dowager had come to seek her out on the beach had held the further surprise of finding him sitting in her parlour, drinking tea and eating *her* teacakes. But of course, it only made sense that the dowager would have been accompanied, especially on such a long journey. Still, though, Jane thought kindly of him to have clearly agreed to devote so much of his time to her avail. But then, in the course of their journey, Jane had discovered just how kind indeed was Robert. She could see why Phillip trusted this man so.

To keep her hands from delivering some respite to her posterior, Jane rubbed her stomach, smiling when she felt the baby kick.

"You look exhausted," the viscount quietly said. "Phillip is going to be ill pleased that we've coerced you into making such a lengthy return to Greystone Hall, but he'll be so happy when he discovers that you are with child." The viscount stretched out his long legs and smiled.

"Do you really believe so?" but the question only hung in the air between them, until Jane said, "He warned me that he didn't want children. He was quite adamant about it." She rested her hands on her stomach, as though protecting her baby.

Robert's gaze followed the movement of her hands. "I've known Phillip a long time and feel certain that if he didn't want children, you wouldn't now be carrying his child. The man I know can't be shaken once he's decided upon a course of action."

The viscount smiled. "Phillip must have had a very good reason to change his mind. I suspect he decided he couldn't imagine a life in which you were not a part."

Heat rushed to Jane's face but she still couldn't resist smiling. She needed to stop doubting the promises Phillip had whispered into her ear whilst holding her tight each night. But his prolonged absence had made it so hard to hold onto that belief.

"I wish I knew for certain you were right." Jane looked down at her quickening stomach and sighed. "I'm so happy to be having Phillip's child. It would break my heart if I thought he didn't want this baby."

She tucked a stray curl of her steadily more un-tidy hair behind her ear, marvelling at how Robert's always looked at its best.

The man then smiled as he regarded her kindly. "He's going to be ecstatic, I'm sure."

"I can't wait to see him again. I thought all I ever wanted was my cottage and to be left alone, but then Phillip filled its rooms with his presence. There's not a one that I can't feel him in, and it only makes me miss him all the more. I used to sit on the beach for hours and watch the waves roll in, content with that, but now they make me wish he was there with me."

Of course Jane couldn't say out loud what she really missed: the way Phillip couldn't keep his hands from touching her, how eventually she would beg him not to stop. Those were memories she cradled next to her heart, ones that kept her awake at night wanting what she hadn't known she missed until Phillip had come into her life.

But then another worry displaced all others. "What if Phillip doesn't make it back home in time for the ball? Society's speculations about our marriage will then only become worse and this whole journey will have been for nothing."

The viscount worked the muscles in his neck at

first, but then said, "We have three weeks. I'll saddle up and ride to London soon after arriving at Greystone Hall. I won't stop looking until I find him. I know where Phillip had originally intended going. He'd heard that Reuben had planned sailing to France for a short stay there. Maybe he set sail before Phillip could reach him. I doubt my friend would just wait around for him to return, though, just kicking his heels, so I'm sure he'll have set sail in pursuit."

"Would he go to such trouble to find his cousin?"

"If being relieved of his title meant Phillip could finally find happiness with you, then yes, I believe he would sail to the ends of the earth if need be." Viscount Worthington's crystal blue eyes all but disappeared, so broad was his smile.

Even after five days in their chilly carriage, Jane hadn't yet become immune to his deep dimples and sweet smile. How had this man not yet been snatched up by some lucky woman?

"Are you sure Phillip really does wish to pass his title to Reuben? There are men who would kill for such a position and the prestige it brings, and I'm not at all sure why he feels it necessary. If he had only asked me, I would have agreed to stay with him at Greystone Hall. I love my cottage, but I love Phillip far more and would gladly live with him wherever he might choose."

The dowager now opened her eyes and straightened her bonnet. "Has Phillip told you anything about his childhood?"

Jane shook her head. "Very little. I did ask him, but he was always hesitant to reveal too much of what his father did to him, and to you, of course. I think he believed it would be a betrayal of your confidence."

"One gets used to not talking about the most important things in one's life, simply because it's just not done." The dowager looked out of the window. "I lived with Reginald's mistreatment because isn't that what a wife does? Stays and says nothing."

The dowager turned her attention back to Jane. "My parents were so excited when Reginald asked for my hand in marriage. My father had heard all the rumours about his bad temper and his being a drunkard. Unfortunately, Reginald's rank rode roughshod over any concerns my father may have had."

She closed her eyes. "And all I saw was how handsome he was. Since I was never allowed more than a few minutes in his company, how could I have been expected to know his true character?"

She now stared at a spot somehow above Jane's head. "It was such a relief that Phillip was a boy. I just couldn't have faced bringing a girl into that house, knowing how Reginald would have hated her as much as he hated me."

Silence filled the carriage as the dowager clearly became lost in her own thoughts, then she said, "The truth of it is that I never wanted to bring any children into my hell," and only then did she meet Jane's eyes once more. "And it was hell, my dear. It seemed that every day Reginald found a new way to terrorise us. I can't tell you how happy I was when Phillip was old enough to be sent off to boarding school. At least that got him away from Greystone Hall for most of the year. But I missed him so; with all my heart."

"Was there no one to help you?" Jane could feel her mother-in-law's pain but refrained from reaching over and taking her hand, for the dowager had drawn within herself, now seemingly untouchable.

Presently, she glanced at Jane and smiled. "My sister, bless her goodness, offered me respite whenever Reginald would let me get away from Greystone Hall, but it had to be with his express permission. He could be very vindictive otherwise, and why Phillip and I walked a very fine line in that household."

Robert turned slightly and took the dowager's hand.

She smiled at him. "Phillip would have been lost without you, Robert. You have no idea how much it meant to him to be able to spend the holidays at your home. He was able to see what it meant to be amongst a real family. And he loved your father so much, but then, in a way it made it harder for him to come home to his own."

The dowager reached across with her free hand and took Jane's. "I know you've heard the rumours that Phillip killed his father." She pursed her lips, clearly remembering that awful time. "I had a feeling the night before that Reginald was planning something. It was just a feeling, you understand, but enough that I kept a close eye on him, just in case he tried to harm Phillip."

She closed her eyes and tightened her grip on Jane's fingers. "On that day, Jane, Phillip saved my life." A small shiver ran visibly through her. "So whatever the gossipmongers may say about my son, their wagging tongues will not speak the whole truth."

The dowager swallowed and squeezed Jane's hand yet tighter still. "Thank God you," she said, briefly turning to Robert, "and Phillip came back from hunting when you did."

That Robert had been with Phillip and the dowager that day of the murder was something Jane had not known before. She glanced at the man, noting how he now clenched his jaw.

"Reginald had been drinking all day; drinking and brooding. I expected him finally to pass out, as he often did, but I think that day he somehow registered that I'd had enough."

She released both their hands and leaned against the back of her seat. "My sister had bought me a small house, and her husband had promised his protection were I ever to leave Reginald. I had already packed my bags when Robert and Phillip came calling upon us, so I put off leaving. I knew it would only be a matter of time before Reginald got to hear of my intention from one of the servants. Few other than my maid could really be trusted."

The dowager closed her eyes, and for a moment Jane thought she'd drifted off to sleep, but then she reopened them and held Jane's gaze in her own.

"Reginald waited until Phillip and Robert had gone hunting before he came looking for me. I had my hiding places, though." She twisted her fingers together and drew in a deep breath. "I think it must have made him angrier still that particular day that he couldn't find me, so by the time he discovered me in the rose garden summerhouse he was incensed."

She let her eyes close again, as though shutting out the memory, and drew in another ragged breath. "Reginald had one of his family's swords in his hand, jabbing it towards me as he raged against my many supposed misdemeanours, then he lunged...just as Robert and Phillip came into the garden."

A shudder ran through the dowager. "Phillip leapt in between us, the tip of the sword slicing across his face. There was so much blood. So much that I froze at the sight of it, but then my motherly instinct threw me across him, across my wounded son, as that beast of my husband raised his blade again, his eyes burning like coals." She stared through Jane, at some far distance, before seeming suddenly to see her. "Then a shot rang out...the deafening shot of a gun."

Jane looked between the dowager and Robert, but then held her mother-in-law firmly in her gaze. "But... But I thought Phillip killed his father. How could he have shot him if you had thrown yourself across him?"

The dowager turned to Robert, drawing Jane's

gaze that same way.

Robert averted his face and looked out of the window of the coach. "Because it was I who killed Phillip's father."

Chapter Nineteen

Jane closed her eyes and pretended to be in her sandy cove, but each time she did so, the mad flurry around her brought her straight back to reality. The dowager duchess's seamstress's endless chatter pulled Jane firmly from her peaceful beach and rooted her in one of the many guest bedchambers.

"This will go faster if you would only stop fidgeting." Mademoiselle Blanchet stopped from pinning up the hem of her latest creation long enough to glare at Jane from her knelt position.

Jane drew in a deep breath and tried not to glare down in return. What was the point, anyway? No one listened to anything she had to say. She had told the dowager at least a hundred times that she didn't need such a large new wardrobe but here she was, being fitted for yet another gown.

Her back hurt and the baby was again kicking, and did the woman never shut up? Did anyone of those here know what the little seamstress was talking about? She kept switching between English and French as if they were interchangeable, and after each sentence, smiled up at Jane, to see if she agreed. What could Jane do but smile and hope a reply wasn't expected.

But more to the point, if the prattling woman stuck one more pin into her again, Jane might very well run from the room screaming. She had no idea why the dowager thought she needed all these new clothes. The lovely sapphire creation for hers and James' wedding celebration would have been enough, but where was she ever going to wear this crimson affair?

Jane tugged at the flimsy gown's non-existent neckline and received another string of what she was almost certain were French profanities from the ever-so-prim Mademoiselle Blanchet. The dressmaker's dainty appearance disguised the heart of a gutter rat, though, and Jane wasn't afraid to admit the dressmaker scared the living daylights out of her. So, in the name of cowardice, Jane stood still and prayed the whole ordeal would soon be over.

"You'll never guess who's just ridden up!" The dowager said as she rushed into the room, a smile lighting up her face. She grabbed Jane's hands and pulled her out of Mademoiselle Blanchet's grasp. The sound of ripping fabric and French swear words followed the two of them out of the room.

Before long they were down the grand staircase and approaching the hall's monumental entranceway. But then the doors swung open and Jane stopped dead in her tracks, leaving the dowager to slip her hand from Jane's as she ran towards the newcomers. "Phillip! Robert!" she called in pure joy.

Too stunned to move, Jane remained rooted to the marble floor, her hands absently clasped over her bump. Over his mother's head, Phillip's eyes met hers, but then travelled down to her proud belly. Jane's heart missed a beat waiting for his reaction, and only when he smiled did she dare breathe again.

Phillip released his mother and hurried over, touching Jane's cheek. His eyes drank her in as though unsure she was really there before him.

"I did not mean to worry you so." He glanced over his shoulder at his friend, now standing uncertainly in the doorway. "Robert's been bending my ear the entire ride back, telling me I should be taking better care of my lovely wife."

Phillip placed his other hand on the curve of Jane's stomach. "He never said anything about a babe, though." His eyes soon met hers again.

Jane lowered them and stared at her fingers, caressing the mound of her stomach. "Perhaps Robert was afraid you might not come back if he had."

Keeping his palm on her stomach, he whispered, "What did I tell you the night before I left?"

She swallowed hard and met his intense gaze with one of her own. "You told me you loved me, but..." Jane glanced down again at the hand still on her belly, "but then I woke up and found a note where you should have been."

He lifted her chin and leaned in, so his face was but mere inches from hers. "But I said I'd be back."

Her chin quivered under his finger. "But then you didn't, and...and you'd already told me several times that you didn't want children." She blinked, forcing back tears. "I couldn't bear the thought that you might hate our child." A tear finally slid down her face, but she drew in a deep breath to hold back any more.

Phillip wiped the tear away and then pulled her to him. "I can't think of a more wondrous thing."

"Truly?" Jane placed her palms against his chest, lost in the feel of his heartbeat. She hadn't been aware of how much she missed having his arms around her, not until they were once again holding her in their safe embrace.

He kissed the end of her nose and smiled. "Truly."

He took a step back but didn't release her. "I'm marring your beautiful new gown with the dust of the road. I could do with a good wash."

His smile turned mischievous. "So what do you say, dear wife? If you help me out of mine, I'll unpin you from yours."

Jane laughed. "Mademoiselle Blanchet might kill us both." She looked up at the fuming woman, now leaning over the bannister and staring down at their reunion.

Phillip pulled her against him once more and whispered, "I'll make it worth your while."

Chapter Twenty

French swearing had followed them into Phillip's bedroom and hadn't stopped until he had thrown the ripped gown out into the hallway. Jane would have gone out to apologise to the dressmaker but Phillip had wrapped his arm around Jane's waist and kissed her until she no longer cared.

Hours later, Phillip snuggled his face into the curve of Jane's neck, making it all but impossible for her to concentrate on anything other than the feel of his warm breath on her neck.

"We need to get up soon. We have to dress for the ball," Jane mumbled, but lost all train of her thoughts when he trailed kisses down her throat and onto her stomach, resting his ear against it.

After a moment he raised his face in surprise. "The little bugger kicked me."

Jane laughed at his comical expression. "He's quite active these days." Then she whispered, "I think he hates your mother's dressmaker, or maybe her French accent. I know it's worn on my nerves these past few weeks."

Phillip pressed his lips on her stomach again before asking, "Do you think he knows I'm his father?"

Jane ran her fingers through his hair, pushing it out of his eyes. "I think he does."

A knock sounded on the door and the dowager's voice called out, "Mademoiselle Blanchet has taken her sewing basket and stormed out, so it's safe for you to come out now, Jane."

There was a short pause and then another knock. "I do hope the two of you are in there getting ready. The guests will be arriving before long."

Another pause. Another knock. "If you need my lady's maid to help you dress and style your hair, just pull on the bell cord and she'll be straight to you."

Another pause and then a loud sigh. "Phillip, do be a gentleman and let you wife get out of bed in time for the ball."

There was another loud sigh and then only silence.

Jane and Phillip looked at each other and giggled. She finally nudged his shoulder. "We had better get up and prove to the world that we are really together as man and wife."

Phillip sat up and slipped off the bed. "I can't believe all the trouble your stepmother has stirred up. I thought, once I had you out of her house, she would leave you alone."

Hating the thought of leaving the comfort of the bed, Jane closed her eyes. "I assumed that once their physician had examined me and told them I was with child, that would have been the end of it. I should have known better."

Fearing the dowager would make a reappearance, Jane leaned up on one elbow and looked over at the sapphire gown. "So what do you know about styling hair."

Phillip leaned over her and nipped the bottom of her ear with his teeth. "I know how to take the pins out."

Jane pushed him back, even though her instincts all but screamed to pull him back into bed. She laughed. "So you've demonstrated."

She stood, went over to the dresser and peered into its mirror, to view the damage. Just as she feared, her blacks curls stood out in all directions. It was going to take a miracle to look presentable in the little time they had, but it was hard to regret the time spent with Phillip in their bed. Just thinking about having him back sent a warm flush through her.

Jane wrapped her arms around herself and sighed. She was certain she would never get used to being so cherished.

Hearing carriage wheels crunching on the gravel outside broke Jane's reverie. "Your mother's going to come back soon. What do you say to playing my lady's maid again and helping me into my new gown?"

He kissed her bare shoulder. "I'll help you if you help me."

Goosebumps covered her arms when he lifted the hair from her neck and touched his lips there.

"I've been wanting to do that ever since I first saw you." He kissed the back of her neck again, then whispered, "And it's just as wonderful as I thought it would be."

Jane sighed and wished they could stay here. Why should they prove anything to people they didn't care anything about?

"Will you protect me from Violet tonight? I didn't have the heart to tell your mother how much your neighbour likes tormenting me at these events."

She stepped out of Phillip's arms and went over to where her gown was hanging. She slipped it over her head and turned her back so Phillip could button it for her.

"I promise to stay by your side all night." He nipped her ear again. "For the right price I could even throw a bowl or two of punch at her, just to repay her for all the times she's drenched you."

It was a tempting offer. "I guess we shouldn't ruin your mother's ball. She's worked so hard to make it a grand event. I think she's really looking forward to it."

When he'd finished fastening the last button, he kissed her neck again. "So how do you go about pinning up a lady's hair?"

Jane grabbed her comb and motioned him away. "Go put your trousers on. I'll just tie my hair back. It will give society something else to talk about." In the mirror's reflection, she watched him pull on his dress trousers whilst she untangled her hair.

"It's dreadful news about your cousin. Are you certain it was him?" she asked as she sorted through her ribbons and finally found one almost the same colour as her gown. Jane slipped it under her hair and met Phillip's eyes in the mirror.

He shrugged. "The French authorities let me see his body and make arrangements to have it brought home."

Phillip slipped on his shirt before meeting her eyes again. "It's a sad affair, going on tour only to be knifed for the few shillings in one's pockets. While we were never very close, it was still such a shock seeing his body." He grimaced. "It made me realise just how lucky I am. I've been so busy running away from this title that I never considered all those who depend on me to perform my role as befits my position. People may starve if I don't manage my estates properly."

Phillip's eyes rested on the bulge of her stomach. "And to think, I almost gave away my son's inheritance. It was wrong of me to try."

Jane rested her hand on her stomach. "You do realise I may be carrying a girl."

He smiled. "I know, and if you are, I'll love her just as much."

Jane smiled but then ran over to the window at the sound of yet more carriages arriving. She pulled the curtain aside and moaned. "We really do need to hurry before your mother sends up a servant to unlock the door and drag us downstairs. She really can be quite ferocious when she's a mind to be."

Phillip laughed and held out his cravat. "What do you know about tying one of these?"

"As much as you knew about styling hair. Go find your valet. At least one of us should be presentable tonight. I'm going to find my slippers and make my way down. Your mother's probably having a fit of the vapours waiting for us to appear."

He walked over and helped her finish tying her

hair back. "You look lovely. Don't you want to wait to go down together?"

She wrapped her arms around him and pressed the side of her face to his chest before pushing him away and stepping out of his reach. "Meet your mother and myself at the door as soon as your cravat is tied, then we'll slay these dragons together."

Jane stopped before opening the door. "When this farce is over, may we go home? I miss sleeping in my own bed."

Phillip laughed. "You can't fool me. You're missing your hidden cove."

He came over and pulled her to him. "I can't wait to go back, either. There are still a few things we haven't done on your beach."

A wonderful warmth spread through Jane's body and she wrapped her arms around him again. "There's more?"

He pressed his face into her neck. "So much more."

Chapter Twenty-One

Phillip watched Jane slip out of the room before pulling the cord to summon his valet. He would have given his right arm to forgo the entire event and stay tangled up in the sheets with his new bride. She was a treasure he had never thought he'd possess and every moment away from her was sheer torment. The hardest thing he had ever done in his life was to leave her to go in search of his cousin.

To help him through his months without her, he had taken to using her trick of closing her eyes, but instead of visualising the cove he saw only Jane, her black mane spread out over white sheets and her ever-changing grey eyes begging him to teach her more about lovemaking. That was what had got him through the demanding journey from Weymouth to Greystone Hall, then on to London and finally France, before the long return here. Of course, the return had been the hardest, knowing it had all been for nothing. And then there had been his best friend bending his ear the whole time, telling him what a fool he had been for leaving his adored wife to face their scandal-seeking society alone.

But then Phillip had thought Jane safe there in

her beloved cottage by the sea. He should have known her stepmother wasn't going to go quietly into the night. People like her seldom did. They were like cats hunting their playthings. It was all just a game to them, the pain they caused of little matter.

Phillip was staring into the mirror, seeing nothing, when his valet knocked and slipped in at his call, carrying his coat and shoes.

"I have pressed your jacket and shined your shoes, milord." Geoffrey held up both items, as though Phillip needed the confirmation of seeing them.

The man was a little too stuffy for Phillip's liking, but he did know how to tie a respectable cravat. He held the very item up in front of Geoffrey as he surveyed his jacket and shoes. "Splendid. If you'd work your magic, I'll then slip into those and go rescue my beautiful wife from our invited vipers."

Geoffrey carefully placed the jacket on its stand and the shoes on the rack below before taking the cravat from Phillip's hand.

But then the valet cleared his throat. "If you don't mind my saying so, your Grace, your good lady wife, the duchess, is the loveliest of women, one who brings such a breath of fresh air to Greystone Hall."

"Thank you, Geoffrey. I don't mind at all."

He lifted his head, so Geoffrey could slip the cravat around his neck, and before adding, "My wife brings a breath of fresh air everywhere she goes. I am indeed a lucky man."

Chapter Twenty-Two

Jane leaned against the bedroom door to steady her nerves, delaying making her way downstairs. She wasn't looking forward to this ball, but the dowager had gone to such a lot of trouble on their behalf. So the least she could do was attend and try her best to remember all the rules of etiquette her tutor had attempted to drill into her head over the years.

To slow her breathing Jane counted to twenty and thought about the way Phillip had done his best to kiss every inch of her since returning home. That thought made her smile but brought her close to opening the door and asking him to do it all over again. Really, who needed a night amongst society's supposed best when her husband was only a few feet away with such strong hands and talented lips?

Jane fanned her face and smiled, but then pushed herself away from his door. Had her stepmother been right? Had she really turned into a wanton hussy, but for some reason the thought only made her giggle.

By the time Jane approached the head of the main staircase, she'd regained her composure, but stopped just short of reaching it.

"Violet." Too stunned to do anything but utter the name of her nemesis, Jane glanced back down the hallway behind her, wishing she'd agreed to go down as a couple.

"The dowager sent me to find you," the hateful young woman smiled, as if she hadn't spent the last three years making Jane's life a living hell. How could it be that such a beautiful woman had such a black heart?

Naturally, good manners won over Jane's desire to snub Violet, and so she smiled in return. "Well, here I am."

Violet scrutinised Jane's new gown, then her hastily assembled hairstyle. "Good lady's maids are so hard to come by these days."

Jane resisted the urge to check her hair ribbon was still in place.

She jutted her chin out and tried her best not to let her temper get the best of her. "But then, of course, some of us need them more than others."

Jane glanced back down the long hallway behind her once more before grasping the handrail. "I'm well aware that my mother-in law-is waiting, so perhaps we should go straight down, before she sends some-one else to look for me. Soon, we will have all the guests up here instead of in the ballroom."

Violet laughed, but hollowly. "That would be a little eccentric, would it not? But then, I suspect everything you do is...shall we say, somewhat unconventional."

Jane descended the long, winding staircase, wishing Violet was not beside her. She remembered the last time they had done this together, when Jane had stumbled and tumbled down the last few steps, ruining the rest of her evening.

"You know Phillip was promised to me," Violet's obnoxious voice presently informed her.

Jane turned and held the handrail. She clasped her other hand to her stomach and was rewarded with the feel of her baby's soft kicks, that wonderful gift helping slow her rapidly beating heart.

"I don't understand what I ever did to make you dislike me so." Jane looked over Violet's shoulder and wished Phillip would hurry, so she didn't have to face this vindictive woman alone.

An evil gleam appeared in Violet's eyes, one that put Jane on edge and made her wish for once she hadn't had so much etiquette drilled into her. Why weren't young ladies ever told how to defend themselves from such bullies?

Violet laughed but glanced over her shoulder before saying, "At first you were merely a source of amusement, but now you're standing in the way of *my* happiness." She leaned forward and spat her next words into Jane's face: "Phillip's mine, and I don't like others taking what's mine."

Jane drew in a deep breath and did her best to remain calm. "Well, I'm afraid you're just going to have to get over it. I'm his wife and his duchess, and I have no intention of allowing that to change. So, perhaps you should find your wrap and leave this ball," and she leaned menacingly nearer Violet, making it clear she was serious. "This is mine and Phillip's ball, given by *my* mother-in-law, to celebrate *our* marriage. So, either go and search out someone else to be your husband or leave. I care not, either way," and without a further glance at Violet, she started to descend the stairs once more. Jane was now in her own family's home and had no intention of putting up with this foul woman any longer.

Jane had only taken a couple of steps when the push came. She grabbed the handrail but her hand slipped when another sent her stumbling further, her arms flailing as she finally sailed through the air like a rag doll. She would have screamed had she not hit the steps on the way down, forcing the breath from her lungs. Dazed, she eventually lay in heap at the bottom of the staircase and looked back up at a smugly smiling Violet, before everything went black.

Chapter Twenty-Three

Phillip cradled his tiny son in the palm of his hands, where he sat beside Jane's bed, and tried hard to memorise the motionless baby's face. Soon after the poor mite's birth, for a short time at least, his son had looked up at him, as if recognising his father.

They had kept their eyes locked, acknowledgment there, until the tiny child's eyes had slowly closed over and he had drawn his last breath.

Tears rolled down Phillip's face now. This was his fault. Why hadn't they gone down together? Jane must have lost her footing on those damned marble stairs.

For a moment anger replaced his broken-hearted despair. He would have workmen there first thing in the morning, tearing the stairway down to replace it with wood.

Phillip was well aware that his mother hovered nearby, the only person he would eventually hand his son to now that the end had come. But for the moment, he was determined to remember every tuft of black hair and his son's perfectly rounded face.

He glanced across at Jane, where she still lay, slipping in and out of consciousness. But even though the doctor had reassured them she would likely make a full recovery, Phillip still worried. He so wished she were awake now, though, long enough to lay her own eyes on this beautiful yet brief fruit of their loving union, long enough to know their son at least in memory.

He could not bear that his firstborn child might be consigned unto the earth without Jane having ever held him. No, not her, not she who had lovingly carried their son for so long, before Phillip had even known he existed. It should have been Jane holding him now as his spirit slipped away into God's safekeeping. What unfair treachery of life was this that she had missed looking into his eyes, that she'd not seen him look back at her?

Phillip touched his lips to his son's forehead, then to his cheeks and finally his mouth. He then gently placed him on Jane's chest.

"You gave me a beautiful son." He leaned over and kissed Jane's forehead. "We'll call him Thomas, after my great-grandfather."

Phillip carefully slid onto the bed beside Jane and their son, and slipped his arms around them both, cradling them, all too aware he had failed as their protector.

Even though Jane couldn't hear his words, he whispered, "You would have liked mother's grandfather. He was so kind to me. There were times when I used to pretend he was my father."

He caressed his son's cheek. "He was everything my own father was not."

As Phillip cupped his son's face, Jane lifted her hand and touched his. He looked down and saw that her eyes were open.

At first, all Jane did was stare at the tiny head slowly rising and falling on her chest, then touched her baby's face before running her fingers through his hair.

A moan slipped from her lips, and Jane cradled her hands around her baby son's face as she hummed a soft lullaby.

Quietly, Phillip's mother drew near, standing beside the bed, and all three hummed the tune of the lullaby to Thomas.

Presently, Jane stopped and turned her eyes to Phillip. "It was my fault. She pushed me once before. I should have known she would again," but as tears ran from her eyes, all Phillip could do was stare in horror.

Still troubled from having watched Thomas's tiny

casket being placed in the wall of the Radcliff vault, Phillip walked aimlessly from room to room. How many times had he hidden in each of these when trying to stay out of his father's reach? He knew each and every cubbyhole and secret passage—something that should have been a game of excitement for any child, but that had been for him a way of surviving into adulthood.

From within their ornate frames and through the yellowed varnish of their portraits, hanging there upon the expensively wallpapered walls, Grim ancestors looked down upon Phillip as he prowled beneath them. How he hated each and every one. They only reminded him of his duties: to keep his many properties and estates in good repair for the benefit of both his own family and those of his tenants who occupied his hundreds of inherited acres.

This rambling hall had never felt like home until Jane came into his life, and now even those wonderful memories had been tainted by the accursed Violet.

After discovering Rueben to be dead in France, Phillip had thought that maybe, with Jane by his side, he could bring some happiness to this huge pile, but what he wouldn't now give to tear this place down with his bare hands, stone by stone.

Phillip wanted to scream and curse but only continued his aimless and silent roam through each room. The last thing he wanted was to wake Jane. It had taken her a long time to fall into each troubled sleep, but each time he had stayed by her side until she had, only leaving once he'd assured himself that the sleeping draughts had taken effect.

Finally, almost too tired to walk, he found himself in his study, but where the sight that met him froze him in its doorway. It had slipped his mind, in all that had happened since Jane's fall, that he'd ordered what had been left of that evening's spirits be brought here to be made ready for disposal. He now bemoaned having relaxed his ban on such supposed enjoyments for the duration of the event.

Phillip opened one of the brandy decanters and sniffed. His hollow laughter, though, only joined the sound of breaking glass, from where he'd thrown the decanter against the wall.

But then something else shattered, something in Phillip himself, and he could no longer contain his tears. Each bottle then found itself hurled at the wall, the study quickly filling with the smell of expensive rare vintages. And now he realised, realised that the one overriding reason he had never wanted children no longer held its power over him. All those wasted years fearing he would be no better than his father, and here he was, in the very worst moment of his life, and not a one of those bottles had called his name.

Finally, Phillip sank into his desk's chair and stared blindly across the room at the glistening stain of brandy on the wall opposite, seeing only Thomas's sweet face. He remembered the moments before the poor babe's death when he'd touched his finger to the child's small cheek , when he'd watched as his short-lived son's mouth curled into a half smile. From it had grown two of the tiniest of dimples, ones that had etched their place for ever in Phillip's heart.

He wiped away his tears, still without seeing, re-membering only that sweet, sweet smile. The one Jane had never seen, he reminded himself, and which omission now haunted him above all else. Phillip hadn't been able to bring himself to tell her about it, not knowing what further hurt it may have brought her, yet another loss to mourn.

"Phillip?" Robert's voice echoed from beyond the office doorway.

Ignoring the mess he only now recognised around him, Phillip dragged himself from his study, in the hope that his good friend might be bringing some tidings that would at least shine a glimmer of light into his darkened heart.

He found Robert with the local magistrate, both standing in the entrance hall. "Robert? Christopher?" but when neither said anything, he demanded, "Well, did you arrest her?"

Robert glanced at the magistrate before slowly shaking his head. "The earl must have known, Phillip. He's sent her away to London."

"So what are you waiting for?"

"The magistrate had a better idea."

"Quick then, we're losing time. What idea?"

The magistrate cleared his throat. "As soon as I heard what the earl had done, I sent my best man to ride after Lady Violet." The man briefly looked down and shuffled his dusty boots. "I hope I didn't overstep my authority, but I told Wilson not to come back until he had her under arrest." He cleared his throat again and his cheeks reddened. "I also told him you would pay whatever expenses he incurred along the way."

Too frustrated to speak, Phillip only ground his teeth. All he wanted to do was throttle Violet until her eyes bulged from her blackening face, but instead, he ran his hands through his hair and paced the entrance hall. When he at last had his temper under control, he said, in a quiet and controlled voice, "I don't care how much it costs. I want Violet to pay for her attempt on my wife the duchess's life and for the death of my son."

Chapter Twenty-Four

The constant sound of the carriage wheels only made Jane's head hurt all the more. She might have closed her eyes to help shut off the pain, but every time she did all she saw was her son's face—so still and peaceful. The memory saddened her, brought an anger and a thirst for revenge.

For her whole life all she had ever wanted to do was what was right. Why did that never seem to be enough? People like her stepmother and Violet only used her good nature against her, and in the end it had only brought death to her son.

"You should try and rest." Phillip slipped from his seat and sat next to her.

When he slid an arm around her shoulders, she stiffened. Jane hated that her involuntary reaction may have hurt his feelings, but she no longer had control over her body. The simplest touch from any-one only made her draw further into herself.

Phillip, though, kissed the top her head. "I feel it too."

She turned to face him. "What?"

"The rage. It's trying to claw out of my chest," which part of him he touched as he grimaced. "All I want to do is scream, but here the two of us are, sitting here as if our worlds haven't been turned upside down. And why? Because that's what we've been raised to do."

Hearing him voice her feelings so aptly made Jane feel closer to her husband than she ever had before.

"Will it ever go away?" Even though the last thing she wanted to do was touch another human being, she leant nearer and took Phillip's hand.

He considered their joined hands and squeezed her fingers. "I'm hoping that in time the anger will lessen," Phillip kissed the tips of her fingers, "for otherwise I don't know how we will ever survive living with this much pain."

"I've never wanted to hurt anyone before, but if Violet were here, I would kill her." A knot in her chest eased somewhat at the saying.

She wasn't proud of her murderous thoughts, but since regaining consciousness and finding her baby boy's still body on her chest, all Jane had then wanted to do was hunt Violet down. Each day her rage had only grown stronger and stronger.

Jane met Phillip's eyes. "You and Robert tried."

"A day too late is as good as a lifetime. I can't believe Wellington actually agreed to run off to America with her, though. I'm not surprised his father disowned him. He'll never be able to come back here again. He's given up everything for that woman."

Jane shrugged. "What did he really give up? Not even the spinsters were interested in marrying him. My guess is that he couldn't believe his luck when Violet asked him to run off with her, especially with her father giving them all that money to start all over again. Why wouldn't he agree?"

She looked away before asking, "Do you think he knew what she had done? I always liked him and would hate to think he did know yet still agreed."

Phillip stretched his legs out, as though the carriage had suddenly become claustrophobic. "I don't know. I hope not. I too liked him. Wellington's certainly boorish, but there's not a mean bone in his body. I feel sorry for him, really, being stuck with Violet for the rest of his life."

"We shouldn't be going back to Weymouth. Not now. You have so many responsibilities at Greystone Hall to attend to. I feel like I'm making you choose between me and your life in Derbyshire." She pushed a brown lock of hair away from his eyes. Even with pain eating away at her she still loved the way those brown eyes of his seemed to caress her. They made her feel loved.

"I chose you, so there's no more choosing to be done. I have a good land steward and Robert is staying until Mother is settled at my aunt's." He tucked a curl behind her ear.

She took his hand. "I wish she'd agreed to come with us. There's plenty of room at the cottage, and it would have got her away from all the bad memories."

Chapter Twenty-Four

Jane ran a finger down the length of his scar. "Your mother told me about the day your father was killed. Why did you allow Robert to take the blame?"

He looked away. "I went against Robert's express wishes. He wanted to tell the truth but I didn't want his good name sullied, and so pleaded self-defence." He fingered his scar. "So it's now only you, my mother, Robert, and myself who know the truth."

She lifted his chin and brought his eyes to gaze into hers. "Why? You had to know society would despise you for it."

Phillip shrugged, but the pain in his eyes told her he wasn't as unaffected as he wished her to believe. "It should have been me, Jane. I'd already killed him a million times in my heart. Robert's life shouldn't have been torn apart because of his defence of me. In that last year, Father had been rapidly going downhill. I should have known he was building up to something heinous. He'd wanted Mother and myself dead for years. It was just a case of when he would pluck up the courage."

This time she squeezed his fingers, her heart breaking for him. "You couldn't have known. You were so brave. Most men wouldn't have stepped in front of a sword, even for their mothers."

She again ran a finger down the length of his scar. "You're always putting other people's needs before your own, Phillip, for which, amongst many things, I'm so proud to be your wife."

Tears filled his eyes. "But I wasn't there when *you* needed me most," then he closed his eyes. "I should have been there for you; I should have been there to save our son."

Chapter Twenty-Five

Even bundled into several layers of clothing, the cold seeped through to Jane's bones. She glanced at Phillip, beside her, to see if he was ready to go back, and wasn't surprised to find he no longer looked out across the water toward the horizon but had his eyes closed. It was something she had found him doing more and more since their return to the cottage.

Where did he go to in these moments? Was she losing him? Maybe he was tired of how melancholy she had grown and he needed to escape to some happier place. She couldn't blame him. She wished she could do the same thing herself, but her old ability to escape just by closing her eyes had deserted her. She was far too angry, but standing here and seeing his anguish made her realise just how much she needed to move on, for his sake as well as her own.

Jane slipped her hand through his and pressed her shoulder against his own. "If we are ever to be happy again, we need to find a way to forgive Violet," she quietly said.

Phillip opened his eyes and met hers. "How do I do that when I keep imagining so many different ways of killing her?"

Jane shook her head. "I've done the same thing, too, but we both know we wouldn't be able to bring ourselves to do such a thing, even if we had the opportunity."

She rested her head against his arm and looked out at the water. "I think our best revenge against Violet will be for us to live happy lives. The unhappy and discontented only revel in their own misery. If what she has done to us turns us into miserable people, then Violet will have won. I don't want her to win, Phillip. I don't want that."

She met his eyes again. "Do you?"

Phillip once more closed his eyes, and this time only sighed.

They stood silently for some time, just the wind and the water as their companions, but then Phillip finally said, "No. No, I don't. I've only ever wanted to be happy, my entire life. I knew, deep down I knew, it was possible. Whenever I stayed with Robert and his family, I saw how much they loved and found so much joy in each other. That was all I ever really wanted."

He touched her cheek. "And then I found you and saw I could have you too." He forced a smile onto his face. "I want to be happy again, Jane. Do you think we can ever rediscover it?"

She wrapped her arms around his waist. "In my mind I used to run to this place every time I faced something too hard to bear, but do you know where I run to now?"

Phillip shook his head, his eyes never leaving her face.

"I run to you. Even during the darkest days I ran to you. If you are by my side, I can find true happiness again."

"You humble me, Jane. Do you know that?" and he brushed his lips against hers. "How, then, can I not be happy?"

He rested his forehead on hers and whispered, "I forgive her, but I will still seek justice for our son. If she gets away with this, then what might she do to someone else?"

Jane nodded. "I agree, but today we have to stop hating her. Are we of one mind on this?"

Phillip swallowed hard before finally nodding. "If you can forgive, then so can I."

He pulled her up against him and they stood in silence, until someone called their names. Phillip released her and stepped back. They turned and looked toward the pathway leading home, seeing a man carefully navigating the rocky descent.

"Who is that?"

After a moment, Phillip said, "I think it's Robert. What's he doing here?"

He took her hand and led her towards their friend. "Could something be wrong with Mother? I should have insisted she came with us."

"I'm sure she's fine. Maybe Robert's only come to see how we're getting on. We have stayed longer than we first said we would." For five months they'd walked their beach, hoping each day would be the one they would no longer feel their overwhelming sadness. But each day they'd crawled into bed, still feeling that their hearts might never heal—no closer to facing the real world than the day before.

Upon reaching Robert, their friend first pulled Jane into a huge hug before doing the same to Phillip. But when he stepped back, his face revealed nothing.

"I came as soon as I heard. I thought you would want to know," he told them, meeting both their eyes as he drew in a deep breath.

"Is Mother unwell?" Phillip wrapped an arm around Jane's shoulders.

After catching his breath, Robert finally shook his

head. "I didn't mean to worry you, but I thought you would both want to hear the latest news from America."

Jane wrapped her arm around James's waist, steadying herself. "There's news of Violet?" Her heart felt as though it might leap from her chest but then she remembered her words to Phillip just now, about forgiving Violet. Was her new vow going to be tested so soon?

"Constable Stephens has returned, then?" Phillip tightened his grip on Jane's shoulder.

"He rode straight to Greystone Hall as soon as his ship berthed," but then he paused, his expression giving nothing away. "Violet and Wellington died of cholera before their ship reached America."

Jane took Robert's hand in hers. "The viscount deserved a better ending. I'm sad for his family. I know his sisters loved him very much." She so dearly wanted Violet's death to be the justice she and Phillip deserved, but then, why did she only feel sadder?

Chapter Twenty-Six

"Phillip! Jane! Wake up!"

In Phillip's dream, Robert called his and Jane's names over and over again, and then his mother nudged his shoulder, as she'd always done when as a child he'd refused to get out of bed. Why couldn't they just let him sleep? It was the best he'd had in months.

He snuggled closer to Jane, pressing his nose into the curve of her neck.

"Phillip! Get up. The house is on fire!"

Those words finally wormed their way into Phillip's awareness and he opened his eyes, just as Robert ran into the bedroom.

"Get up. You have to get out of here before the place burns down around our ears." Robert pulled the bedcovers back and grabbed Phillip's arm.

Phillip seized Jane by the shoulders and shook her. "Wake up. The cottage is on fire!"

Jane eyes popped open, still clouded with sleep, but the urgency in Phillip's voice soon got her moving. She slid out of bed and let him push her towards the doorway.

"Where's the fire?" Phillip said, glancing over his

shoulder at Robert who was urging them out into the hallway.

"I heard what sounded like glass breaking, so I went down to see and found smoke coming from the rear of the cottage."

Without warning, Jane stopped directly in front of them both, at the top of the stairs. "Where's Helen?"

Phillip pushed her on, the air now thick with smoke, afraid that if they didn't get out soon, they never would. "Once we've got you safe, Robert and I will go around the building to check," and they went down the stairs into far hotter air.

"It's too early for Helen and Silas," Robert said behind them. "It's still dark out there."

Jane stumbled near the foot of the stairs, but Phillip grabbed her gown, steadying here but ripping its thin fabric. As they huddled together in the hall, Phillip stared through the thickening smoke, finally making out the front door, towards which he shoved Jane. She briefly fumbled with its handle, but then they were all safely outside in the fresh air, coughing and spluttering.

"I'll just go around to the rear and see if Helen's anywhere to be seen," Phillip managed to say, then pointed at the adjoining stables. "Robert, you go turn the horses out into the paddock."

Jane grabbed his arm. "What should I do?"

In his relief at them now being safely outside, Phillip pulled her up against his chest and kissed her soundly on the lips. "Come with me. I don't want you out of my sight."

What he didn't want was her going back in to save any of her precious possessions, like the portraits of her mother and grandmother in the hall, two items at least she might think worth risking her life for. Before she might remember them, Phillip took Jane's hand and rushed her to the rear of her now clearly burning cottage—the very place she cherished above all others.

Chapter Twenty-Seven

"So, has the constable been able to get him to talk yet?" Jane gathered up her borrowed gown, so she didn't trip over it as she followed Phillip. Helen and Silas had been kind enough to put the three of them up for the night, although it was a bit of a tight squeeze in their small cottage. Her housekeeper would have also lent Jane a dress but the woman weighed at least a good four stone more than her, so one of her thinner neighbours had been kind enough to lend Jane one.

Phillip looked over his shoulder, noticing she'd fallen behind, and so slowed his pace.

"Robert and Constable Brown tried last night to see if they could get the man to tell them who'd paid him to set the fire, but he wouldn't say a word to either of them."

"Maybe he's not talking because there's nothing to tell," and Jane drew in a frustrated breath as she again had to lift the hem of her dress. It was far too tempting just to shed it and finish the walk to the village in her night shift. There were, she once again concluded, some serious drawbacks to being a woman. What she wouldn't give to be able to walk around in a shirt and trousers. She hated every single layer women were forced to wear.

Phillip stopped and waited for her to catch up, then offered his arm. "Both the constable and Robert believe the man had too many coins in his pockets for someone dressed so shabbily."

Jane gratefully accepted his offered arm. "But why do you think he had anything to do with the fire?"

"He would have gone unnoticed if he hadn't sought out the local doctor, to do something for his burns." Phillip waited for Jane to gather her skirts into her other hand before setting off again.

"Maybe he was one of the men who had come to help put out the fire." All their efforts, though, had been in vain, and despite everyone's best attempts, the cottage had been gutted, everything of her mother's now gone forever.

Jane blinked back her tears and worked hard not to dwell on what had been lost, to remember what she still had. Thanks to Robert, she and Phillip were still alive, and the longer they were together, the more certain Jane became that they could overcome any-thing as long as they had each other. The fire had re-turned her the Phillip she had married—the fearless man she knew him to be. The man who was now clearly determined to get to the bottom of who had tried to kill them.

Once they'd been able to get into the remains of their burnt out cottage, Robert had found remnants of at least three lanterns where the kitchen had stood, clearly what Robert had heard being thrown through a window. Whoever had done it, they had plainly been set on killing them as they slept in their beds.

"Let's go see if the man's up to talking today. The blackguard was feverish yesterday from his injuries."

Phillip eventually brought them to the door of a two storey townhouse at the centre of the village. Tiny yellow flowers were just beginning to break forth from their buds in the tidy front garden, giving the otherwise dull Spring scene some much needed colour.

An short, angular man answered the door.

"Ah, good morning, Your Grace, milady. The constable said you might well visit today," and he invited them inside, where Phillip shook the doctor's hand.

"Good to meet you at last, Doctor Wainwright. I was hoping your patient would be up to talking to us today."

"Indeed, Sir, but I must trust to your own discretion in knowing when our Mister Smith may have had enough. Frankly, it is my opinion that the man is unlikely to last the day out. His burns are too extensive for my skills to be of much help. He's as comfortable as possible, of course, but I'm afraid it's now out of my hands."

Jane placed her own hand on the doctor's arm. "Would you be so kind as to take us to him?"

The patient didn't even open his eyes when they entered the bedroom, so Jane quietly sat in the chair nearest the bed, steeling herself to regard the disfigurement of the badly burnt man. He smelled unwholesome, of weeping blisters and body odour. The smell made the small room feel even smaller.

Jane waited until Doctor Wainwright had closed the door behind him before she tentatively enquired, "Mister Smith? My husband and I have called to see how you are. We heard that you were badly hurt in a fire and wished to learn if there was anything you needed."

The man moaned but didn't open his eyes. Phillip's impatient shuffling sounded loud in the small, quiet room, and Jane shot him a look that warned him not to interfere.

"I'm Jane Radcliff, The Duchess of Greystone," she said, relieved when the man's eyes finally opened.

Through his swollen lips, he managed to mutter, "I'm dying, aren't I?"

Jane would have taken one of his hands to offer him some comfort but they were too badly burned, so she merely told him, "I don't know."

The man let out another low moan. "I'm glad you aren't dead. I wouldn't want to go to Hell for having murdered you."

"So you did set fire to my cottage," and she shifted closer, despite the overwhelming stench.

The dying man tried to swallow but only choked. Jane motioned for Phillip to hand her the glass of water on the bedside table. She helped Mister Smith take a drink, but most ran out from the side of his mouth.

He finally met her eyes again. "He paid me to do it. Said to make certain you were good and asleep before I set it, though. He wanted to be sure you went up with it, made me promise before he gave me the money."

No longer able to stand silently by, Phillip asked, "Who did?"

"The Duchess of Blackmore's man."

Chapter Twenty-Eight

"But the duke will only see his own daughter." Phillip jammed his boot against the door then pushed his way into the Blackmore London townhouse, turning to pull Jane inside behind him. Her face was pinched from exhaustion. Even though he had wanted to ride to London without her, she had refused to stay behind in Weymouth.

The butler then tried to closed the door against Robert, but he too forced his way in. "Sorry, chap, but it's raining out here and I'm exhausted." He took off his hat and overcoat before adding, "Be a good man and see to it that the duke and duchess are served a good hot pot of tea and we'll just forget you tried slamming the door in our faces."

As they watched the butler hurry away, Phillip helped Jane remove her jacket before removing his own. "It's probably safe to say we're not going to be enjoying tea any time soon."

He wrapped his arm around Jane's waist. She looked as if she might collapse right there in the hall. Since Thomas's death she had lost weight she could ill afford to lose, not helped now by her having insisted she ride on horseback with them, all that way to her father's townhouse, to save time. She had barely eaten since discovering that her stepmother had paid for her cottage to be destroyed, them along with it.

Jane leaned her head on his shoulder. "I would only choke on anything served to us in this house. What's to say my stepmother wouldn't have laced it with poison?"

"A fair point, my dear." Phillip stood straighter, his arm, though, still about Jane, as her father stormed into the hall, but he appeared thinner, his face more pinched.

"How dare you come into my house uninvited?" he roared, spittle flecking every word.

Phillip stepped between them. "Your wife tried to have us killed, Sir, so you're damned lucky we decided to come here first, not to seek audience at the king's court to pursue our grievance against her."

"How dare you try to dishonour the good name of my wife," and Phillip was surprised to see tears welling in Duke Blackmore's eyes. "Is it not enough that she took her own life last night because of that viper?" and he thrust his arm out towards Jane, his eyes now wild with rage.

Jane recoiled then whimpered in clear distress,

but her father lunged for her.

Phillip savoured the satisfaction of punching him in the nose, the older man staggering back into his trusty butler's arms. Affronted by such intimate contact, Blackmore ungratefully slapped the man across the face before drawing himself up to his full height and looking down his bloodied nose at them. "She killed herself because of you," he screamed, and pulled a piece of paper from his pocket, which he briefly waved at them before slipping it back into his jacket.

"She had another miscarriage," he told them, his voice now wavering. "All she wanted was to have a son for me."

He gave Jane a look that even sent a chill down Phillip's spine, the man clearly unhinged by his loss. Phillip stepped back, wrapping his arm more firmly around Jane. She shivered then turned to meet his eyes. How he wished she'd gone straight to Greystone Hall when he and Robert had started out on this journey . How would she ever forget the mad tirade her father had just delivered, or the crazed gleam that still shone from the man's eyes.

"Your being alive whilst her own babies only withered was all she needed to convince herself that she'd failed me," but then the duke seemed to deflate, as though his will had suddenly deserted him.

"You now know she tried to have us killed," Jane levelled at him, "yet you still take her side?" She dug her fingers into Phillip's side but didn't back down, even pulled them a step or two towards her father. "So there's no confusion, that we're clear in our understanding of each other: you are now dead to me, do you hear? As far as I'm concerned, I no longer have a father and was never your daughter. You, Sir, can consider yourself at liberty to regard me as being dead too, if it so suits your deranged view of your life. After all, your so dutiful wife did try her damnedest to make it so."

Jane raised her chin and stared at the duke. "I cannot, in all honesty, express sorrow at hearing of your wife's demise. At least now Phillip and I can go to sleep at night without worrying what she would have had planned for us next." Without another word, she stormed out of the house.

Phillip motioned for Robert to go with her, then turned to the duke. "Sir, you never deserved your daughter, nor do I think you will ever have the slightest idea of just how much you have lost here today."

He slipped his gloves back on whilst the duke only

stared fixedly at him. "Jane's the best thing that ever happened to me. I cannot conceive of how she avoided the crushing of her spirit you and your wife were so intent upon achieving. Glad I am that she always had her cottage to run off to, even if only in her thoughts."

He made for the door but then paused. "I, Sir, am going to rebuilt it for her, for that is the one place that held her most cherished memories of her mother. It will return her some happiness at least, which is all I need to make me happy in myself. I know you won't understand this, but that's what one does when one truly loves another."

Chapter Twenty-Nine

Since the day they'd left for Weymouth after the wedding breakfast, Jane had never seen the inside of Phillip's London townhouse. Having stayed at Greystone Hall, she assumed it would be just as extravagant, but was surprised to discover it was warm and inviting. The entrance hall had none of the cold marble that ran throughout his country house but was wood-panelled, its staircase beautifully fashioned from mahogany with carved balusters and carpeted steps. Sheer sky-blue curtains hung at the windows and all its highly polished wooden floors were covered in brightly coloured oriental rugs.

As though reading Jane's thoughts, Phillip told her, "Father seldom came with us to London, so Mother had free rein to decorate the house as she wished." He helped Jane out of her coat and handed it and his own to a waiting butler. Robert did likewise.

"John, let me introduce you to my new duchess." Phillip raised Jane's hand to his lips and kissed her fingers. His smile did little to mask how exhausted he was after their long ride from London, but as always, he was ever the gentlemen.

"It is, Lady Radcliff, with utmost pleasure that I

welcome you to his Lordship's house."

The butler had to be seventy if he was a day, a rare thing indeed, and a glowing testament to Phillip's benevolent nature. It brought Jane to love her husband all the more.

"The pleasure is mine, I do assure you, John," but her exhaustion was now getting the better of her, the long day and the emotional stress she'd been through bringing her to slip her arm through Phillip's for support.

Sensing his wife's tiredness and before dismissing the butler, he instructed the man to, "See to it that Misses Watkins has a fire lit and tea is served for us all as soon as possible in the front parlour, if you'd be so kind. Oh, and make sure a maid's laid out fresh linen in mine and our principal guest room."

Phillip tucked his hand through the crook of Jane's arm, further instructing, "You'd better see to having some water heated for the duchess's use before dinner is to be served. She's talked of nothing else but a hot bath for the last day and half," and he smiled at Jane.

Although Jane was sure she'd hardly mentioned the prospect of such a pleasure, hearing Phillip's request made her long for one above all else—that and a good night's sleep. It had been all but impossible to rest since finding out that her stepmother had wished her death. There had never been any love lost between them, but to go so far as to... Well, it didn't bear thinking about.

John offered a short bow, briefly presenting the top of his shiny, bald head. "As you wish, Your Grace."

Jane smiled at him. "Thank you, John. Please tell Misses Watkins that I'm sorry to be such an imposition, especially at so short a notice." She glanced at Phillip, thinking that the journey here had been quite unexpected for them, too.

"I will, milady," and he offered Jane another brief view of his bald head before leaving.

Phillip laughed at Jane's bemused expression. "The last time John wore his wig, it gave him a bad rash, so I told him to throw it away." He patted her hand. "Do you mind that our butler is old and bald?"

Jane laughed. "Of course not. I rather like it." She leaned in closer and whispered, "You do remember that I love breaking as many of society's rules as possible, don't you?"

He chuckled before turning to Robert. "You're staying, of course."

"I couldn't climb back on my horse even if I wanted to. I'll stay the night and go see my family tomorrow, after breakfast." Robert looked at Jane. "I'm sorry it didn't go better with your father."

Jane shook her head. "I'm not. I think it's better to know where I stand with him than always to be guessing whether he really loved me or not. I always thought that maybe if he had never married that awful woman we would have been closer, but I see now he probably never did love me. He wanted a son, which my mother failed to give him, and so he put too much pressure on my stepmother. I can't help but think he's the real reason she killed herself."

She tucked a stray curl of her hair behind her ear. "I can't say my father's lack of love for me hasn't made me sad, because it has, but I know my mother loved me more than life itself."

Jane glanced at Phillip and smiled. "And I have Phillip now. What else could I ever need?"

Phillip hugged her close, but stepped away when someone cleared their throat. "Ah, John?" he said, realising the butler had returned.

Jane was too exhausted to stop herself giggling. Maybe she'd be rested enough the next day to put the façade back in place and act as a duchess should.

"Misses Watkins says, milord, since it is laundry day, that there is already enough hot water for both Your Grace and The Lady Duchess."

"Tell Misses Watkins that she can set a tub in my room and one in the guest bedroom for Viscount Worthington. The duchess and I will make do with the one. And let Misses Watkins know that she can delay tea for a couple of hours."

"Phillip!" Jane whispered, admonishingly. When John had left, she added, "Whatever will Misses Watkins think of me—of us both?"

Phillip laughed and pulled her tight against his chest. "Dear Misses Watkins will only wish she was still young enough and small enough to fit into a tub with a man. So, let's give the woman something to dream about."

Jane buried her face into his jacket and laughed. What a lucky day it had been when she'd accidentally snared this wonderful man—her duke who never acted like one. She hadn't thought him what she wanted, but he'd proven to be just what she'd always needed.

She lifted her face away from his chest, certain it was as red as it felt, and gazed up at him. "Have I told you lately that I love you so? Because I do."

She touched his cheek then kissed him passionately, all too aware they were subjecting poor old Robert to a most vulgar display of affection.

Phillip pulled her even closer, though,. "I love you too, duchess of mine."

He angled a look at his good friend Robert. "I'm finally a lucky man. It's taken me years, but I finally have everything I need, for once in my life."

Robert smiled, clearly wondering if they'd really lost their minds but evidently more than happy for them. "I can see you have, Phillip. I can see that all too clearly."

Jane pushed herself away from Phillip's embrace and took one of Robert's hands in hers. "You won't know this, but for years I fantasised that you were my brother, and that whenever I needed help, you would come rushing to my rescue."

Robert gently squeezed her fingers and looked down at their joined hands. "And from this moment on, that, my dearest friend, is no longer a fantasy. I've always considered Phillip my brother, but also you as my sister from the moment the two of you were married. I'll always be here for either of you, at any time you may have need of me."

Jane kissed his cheek. "And so you have been.

You have no idea how much I've appreciated your kindness and welcomed your help."

She glanced back at Phillip. "We're here for you, too, my dear husband. Whenever you have need of either one of us, all you need do is ask and we'll be there."

Phillip drew her back to him by her hand. "So, now we're all one big family, would you mind," he directed at Robert, "if I take my wife up and help her take a bath?"

Jane hung her head and Phillip laughed.

"A very long and a very hot bath" he quietly told her, but then more loudly to Robert: "Enjoy your own, my brother, and...and if we aren't down in time for tea, please start without us."

Chapter Thirty

"When I've finished with your hair, Caroline, go tell your father it's teatime. Maybe he can get your brother out of the water long enough to eat something." Jane worked at tidying her daughter's long black braid but finally gave up and let her skip off down the beach in search of Phillip and Ian. No doubt both would be elbow deep in sand, giving Helen another reason to fuss over how much of it the two would stomp through the cottage.

Jane patted her swollen stomach, acknowledging the rather hefty kick from within. "Don't worry. Helen will be certain to have enough teacakes laid out to keep us both happy, at least until dinner is served."

She looked up and smiled at the sight of Phillip steering Ian towards her. At least her level-headed daughter had enough common sense to ignore them both, now happily skipping well ahead of them and their usual fray. Caroline loved teacakes just as much as her mother did, and had very early on worked out that the first into the house could have their fill before Phillip and Ian would rapidly devour the lot.

"Can I be given leave to go up now?" Caroline said as she approached. "Father and Ian will be forever getting here. Ian has befriended another make-believe friend. Father's trying to talk him into leaving him on the beach until we come back later, but Ian is insisting he join us for tea." She rolled her beautiful grey eyes, as though to say her little brother was such a trial.

Jane would have laughed at such dramatics but didn't want to belittled her daughter.

"Certainly. Tell Helen we'll be up shortly." Jane pulled Caroline into a close embrace, caressing her cheek, savouring its soft fresh feel. Of course Caroline thought herself far too old for such things, and so, true to form, she soon wriggled free and ran off towards the path back to their cottage.

Jane called after her, "Let your grandmother know we'll be up shortly."

It was impossible to tell whether she'd heard or not, for Caroline never turned once she'd been given permission to leave. Jane laughed at her daughter's unladylike sprint along the beach, something Jane knew full well would have fallen short of society's expectations. Poppycock, she thought, for she just loved seeing how free this treasured place allowed them all to be, the one place where society held no sway. Soon enough it would dictate how her daughter must behave, but until then Jane first wanted her to have a chance to blossom before the inevitable happened. She wanted her children to know she loved them unconditionally, especially here, here on the beach where they could so freely discover pure joy. As it had been for herself when she'd stayed here with her own mother, and now with her own husband and children.

"Mother," a familiar small voice said, "please tell Father that my friend may join us for tea."

Identical pairs of brown eyes stared at Jane, waiting for her verdict. She had to bite her lip to keep from laughing at how similar were father and son, the only difference being that the father had more sand on his face and his hair needed trimming. Maybe Phillip would let her take her sewing scissors to it before dinner, but then, maybe not. The memory of its last such butchering reproachfully sprang to mind.

Jane kneeled, to be at eyelevel with Ian. "So you've made another new friend, have you? And, I take it, one with whom your father is reluctant to share his teacakes?"

She glanced up at Phillip and he winked. To avoid laughing, she looked back at Ian.

The boy's chubby cheeks were red from being out in the sun too long. The poor child had inherited his fair complexion from Phillip's mother. Why wouldn't he keep his hat on, Jane wondered, particularly when he just loved being outside all the time.

"My friend has promised not to eat your teacakes. He just wants to spend time with us, don't you," and Ian stared at the empty space beside him.

"Does your new friend have a name?"

Ian nodded. "He says Father gave it to him."

"Really." Jane met Phillips eyes again, but he only shrugged.

"So, when did your father give your friend his name?" She wiped sand from Ian's nose.

Her son gave her the same look Caroline gave whenever she thought Jane had asked her a silly question—one that clearly said she wasn't as smart as a mother should be sometimes. "When he was born, of course."

By now Jane was certainly interested but also a little confused. "What's your friend's name?"

"Thomas, but you know that already, since he's my big brother." Ian smiled at the spot beside him.

Time stood still for Jane. She rocked back on her heels and met Phillip's eyes.

He, though, kneeled in front of Ian. "Thomas is here?"

Ian nodded. "Of course, where else would he be?"

He held his hand out for Phillip to take, which his father duly did, then turned back to Jane. "Thomas said he'll hold your hand, so you don't fall."

Jane held out her hand towards where Ian had looked. Then, for the briefest of moments, she saw a little boy with black hair, soft grey eyes, a crooked smile and the sweetest of dimples.

She closed her fingers around his, and together they followed Phillip and Ian to the path that led back to their cottage home.

The End

If you enjoyed *I Close My Eyes*, you may also enjoy my contemporary romances.

Concealed in My Heart https://www.amazon.com/Concealed-in-my-Heart-ebook/dp/B00E8828NM/ref=sr_1_7?s=digital-text&ie=UTF8&qid=1375184032&sr=1-7&keywords=regina+puckett

Songs that I Whisper https://www.amazon.com/Songs-that-Whisper-Warren-Family-ebook/dp/B00HVQJFWK/ref=asap_bc?ie=UTF8

What the Heart Knows https://www.amazon.com/What-Heart-Knows-Warren-Family-ebook/dp/B00KJON5G2/ref=asap_bc?ie=UTF8

Love's Great Plan https://www.amazon.com/Loves-Great-Plan-Warren-Family-ebook/dp/B0172QIBZ0/ref=asap_bc?ie=UTF8

Love is a Promise Kept https://www.amazon.com/Love-Promise-Kept-Warren-Family-ebook/dp/B008VTIJUU/ref=asap_bc?ie=UTF8

The Warren Family Series https://www.amazon.com/Warren-Family-Regina-Puckett-ebook/dp/B0173X2RFM/ref=asap_bc?ie=UTF8

Once Upon a Modern Time https://www.amazon.com/Once-Upon-Modern-Regina-Puckett-ebook/dp/B00OJ9M272/ref=asap_bc?ie=UTF8

Regina Puckett is a 2014 Readers' Favorite Award winning author for her sweet romance, Concealed in My Heart. I Will Breathe and Borrowed Wings, both received the Children's Literary Classic Seal of Approval. "I Will Breathe" was also selected as a Science Fiction Finalist in the 2015 IAN Book of the Year Awards, won the bronze in the 2015 Readers' Favorite Book Awards and was the only medalist in the 2016 New Apple Ebook Young Adult Science Fiction category.

She writes sweet romances, horror, inspirational, steampunk, picture books and poetry. There are always several projects in various stages of completion and characters and stories waiting in the wings for their chance to finally get out of her head and onto paper.

Amazon Author's Page http://www.amazon.com/ReginaPuckett/e/B004S3ORSG/ref=dp_by-line_cont_ebooks_1

Website http://reginapuckettsbooks.weebly.com/

Goodreads http://www.goodreads.com/author/show/154116.Regina_Puckett

Google+ Google +
https://plus.google.com/116509703065029920410/

posts

Pinterest Pinterest https://www.pinterest.com/reginapuckett1/

Twitter https://twitter.com/ReginaPucket

Facebookhttps://www.facebook.com/regina.puckett1

Barnes & Noble http://www.barnesandnoble.com/s/regina+puckett

Kobo https://store.kobobooks.com/en-ca/search?query=Regina%20Puckett&fcsearch-field=Author

Made in the USA
Columbia, SC
03 June 2017